The Upsurge

By

G.L. Giles

Author's Note:

Since I had so much fun with the subversive style of writing dialogue without quotation marks in the first edition of "The Upsurge," I decided to follow suit in this second edition.

I have also greatly added to an existing chapter (from the first edition), and I've also added an entirely new chapter-complete with new characters.

Yours in fun-filled dark delight,

G.L. Giles

P.S. Some rather freakish trivia: The first edition of "The Upsurge" was published on September 16, 2018-complete with my fictional Hurricane Willa-and a little over a month later (in October 2018), real-life Hurricane Willa made landfall in Mexico.

CHAPTER ONE (FROM LEE MCPHERSON'S POINT OF VIEW):
"Protagonists Interacting"

You alright, *son*? Mr. Mehia questions, glancing in his rearview mirror at me fiddling with my backpack.

How I wish I were his son sometimes, I first wistfully, then guiltily, think, fiddling with the *TSOL* band button I'd pinned to my backpack when he'd picked me up for school earlier that morning. Now, he was also kind enough to drop me off after it. His son, Luis, and I go to the same private school in Edisto, South Carolina. It's private, but ideas of elite private schools shouldn't come to mind, as it is also country in some aspects. Yep, a somewhat countrified private school where the 'c' might as well be a 'k' while leaving out the 'o,' as in 'kuntrified.'

Mr. Mehia and my father are different in many ways, but similar in others---similar in the ones that probably count the most. Our fathers had bonded at a vegetarian meetup in Mount Pleasant, SC over a year ago, so we, their sons, are expected to get along. Fortunately, we naturally do anyway. And, the monthly veggie get-togethers have become a part of all four of our lives. Even though the hour and a half trip to Mount Pleasant from Edisto is a bit of a downer. So, three hours roundtrip monthly isn't ideal, but most in Edisto aren't exactly enlightened enough to be vegetarians.

Many here aren't even that concerned with human rights. We try to spread the word about speciesism as a type of modern slavery, but it isn't easy.

Sure, I offered, getting back to Mr. Mehia's question, trying to be nonchalant, so as not to show how embarrassed I am at our telltale poverty every time. We live in the country part of Edisto, whereas Mr. Carlos Mehia and his son, Luis, live on the beach part of Edisto in a grand house on the water. They have plenty of money; us, hardly any, though my father had managed, through volunteering for lots of overtime, to save enough to get me into the private school. In fact, as Mr. Mehia traveled down the yawning sprawl of unpaved rural road leading to our place, it is always apparent that his Bugatti Veyron, custom made on the interior with 'pleather,' wasn't exactly suited to all the rocks and holes on the path. Before long, I can see our living quarters: a yurt. Embarrassed every time I am dropped off by him, I quickly dive out of the luxury car. Thanks, see you tomorrow, I shout back behind me, already making tracks between me and their expensive vehicle. I don't want to look back because I don't want to see any pity in Mr. Mehia or his son's eyes. Not that they'd mean to let it show, but I'm a sensitive kid and probably way more aware than I should be for my own peace of mind. Besides, I love my father, through thick and thin, so that momentarily weak thought I'd had about being Mr. Mehia's son was quickly forgotten as soon as I walked in long strides towards our yurt.

CHAPTER TWO (FROM LUIS MEHIA'S POINT OF VIEW): "Beach Mansion Life"

Poor kid, my dad volunteers, looking at me intently. Hope you stand up for Lee at school! Not everyone has it that easy, you know?!

Yeah, I know, dad. Don't worry…we stick together. The other kids think we're both *weird* for being vegetarians, so he has company, I couldn't help grinning.

My dad matched my grin before checking himself with his role as my parent. My sole parent now. Well, it's not weird. It's enlightened.

Eso es, Papa! I agree in a respectful tone, even when using slang.

Sabes que me gusta cuando hablas en espanol, 'mijo'!

Yeah, well, I can't exactly burst out en espanol in school, since there's no need for me to take

Spanish classes and pass it off that way, so I keep it up pretty much only when with you. So, circling back to the enlightened bit: most tenth graders aren't *enlightened* dad, I say, smiling easily across the seat at him, while putting on my wireless high-end headphones to listen to my favorite retro band: Butthole Surfers. Listening to "Pepper" in my left ear while pulling up the right side to be able to still hear my dad, I offer, But don't worry, I have a soft spot for the underdogs with all their ostensible problems. In fact, that's why I had waited until we'd dropped off Lee at his yurt before pulling out my pricey headphones. Lee only has cheap earbuds, so I didn't want to rub my expensive headphones in his face.

Dad is beaming at me for using the word ostensible and focusing on that. Ostensible, son? Words like that used to get me beat up in school, dad smiles broadly.

Yeah, well, I'm not in school right now, so no worries. Besides, I like impressing my dad…es mi porteria…as I get more stuff from him that way, I say with a lopsided smile as I tilt back in my seat, close my eyes and rest…till we arrive at the driveway to our lavish beach house---about 20 minutes from where we'd dropped Lee off at his country place.

I would be lying to myself if not admitting that I am living the 'sweet life' in many ways as I climb up the stairs to the first deck of our beachfront mansion which is the ceiling of our screened-in basement beneath. In that respect, ours is like many of the affluent beach houses here. Our breezy basement houses a deluxe shower, pool table, and an assortment of a dozen or so surfboards. There is also a well-crafted and weather-proofed wooden walkway directly to our own dock at the beach. My dad holds the door open waiting for me to enter into our grand foyer which is a bit out-of-place in a beachhouse. In fact, the only thing that really makes it a 'beach house' is the fact that it is directly on the beach with a magnificent view of the water and houses items you use at the beach. Our foyer has a set of inside stairs which leads up to five bedrooms. Two for us, and three for guests. One of my favorite spots is in our truly great 'great room.' It has windows from the floor to the ceiling with breathtaking views of the ocean. They have hurricane-resistant windows and doors leading out to their decks and patios as hurricanes are no strangers to the area.

Hungry, son? dad asks, on the other side of the long marble bar separating the open-floor plan great room from the spacious kitchen.

You know it, I answer, plopping down on a new ultra-comfy 'pleather' couch with a kind of cutting-edge firm foam. I'd love a loaded veggie burger…thanks, dad.

Pouring a glass of filtered water for himself he asks, So, besides not using the word ostensible, what else happened or didn't happen at your school today? How was it?

Nothing much, and fair to middling, I answered. I fiddled with my backback's zipper a bit, as I didn't want to share with my dad that I'm digging a girl in my class. Her name is Graciela.

I know dad loves me responding with non-hackneyed expressions, even though he probably knows I'm withholding some interesting information, too. Namely, that Graciela is transgender (MTF). Pretty sure my open-minded father would be fine with it, but I am just not ready to share yet. Not because he wouldn't approve, but because I'm not sure that my feelings are reciprocated yet, so I feel that it's best to just chill and say nothing for now. He's seen us talking after school a few times, and he's waved and smiled at her, but I don't think he knows I dig her as more than a friend or that she's trans. Gotta love it when I repeat myself, I smile with a silly grin and shake my head at myself.

Amused at my expression, dad volleys back. Don't know how many colleges will be looking for such *enthusiastic* applicants who describe their days as 'fair to middling.'

Not to be outdone, I respond with, Yeah, well, to be fair, it was just today I described that way. Who knows what tomorrow will bring? Exciting is not always good.

Fair enough, son. Your veggie burger'll be ready in about 15 minutes. You can go to your room. I'll call you down when it's ready.

Dad knows my routine. I go home, talk to him for a bit, then change into my wetsuit, eat, surf, unwind even more by playing Warframe and then do my homework. I have an iPhone X, but I don't really text much (I know: super strange for a kid my age, but not every 'kid' loses their mom at an early age---I grew up quickly in some ways), and I certainly don't actually call on it much. Difficult life, I know. Never said I wasn't a bit spoiled in some ways, too. Maybe in every area of my life, except that one: my mother'd died just a little over three years ago. I would trade every single possession I had just to be with her again---if only for a day.

Dad had us in counselling for a while after her death, and I hated it. I still don't want to talk about her death, and for the most part, dad respects that. Even thinking about my mother's death is making me chew on the inside of my left cheek like some kind of freaky self-cannibal.

Dad, by contrast, handles her death as well as can be expected. Except for the fact that he'd started collecting memento mori artwork: framed paintings, rings, coins, et cetera--- including a walking stick with a skull atop it for a hand grip---even I have to admit it's cool, as it doubles as a sword when it's pulled apart. He keeps it in the trunk of the Bugatti in case his knee starts acting up. He's had it lock up on him a few times and fallen as a result. He'd never been that darksider-like before. At first I thought it peculiar, but now I think it's pretty awesome. And, even with him being my dad, I know he's also a pretty cool cat.

In my room, decked out with framed posters of my favorite surfers riding enormous waves, a Bruce Lee poster and a 100-inch television on the wall not facing the sliding glass doors opening out to a deck with another fantastic view of the ocean, I quickly throw my backback on my gaming chair, and start getting ready to surf. With the water not colder than about 55F, I decide that one of my newer 3/2mm wetsuits is the perfect choice. Like I said, I will play Warframe later on my big television---after surfing but before homework. I know, such a rough life I lead. Yep, I like repeating myself, even in my own mind. The councilor we'd seen said it may be a kind of PTSD after losing my mom.

I miss the days dad used to surf with me after my school. His knee surgery about 9 months ago changed that. That's why his knee sometimes locks up on him. Though he does his best not to let it show that he is extremely bummed out about it. He had to use a walker at first, but now he just walks with a slight limp. He makes jokes to showcase his new limited activity like: let me know if anyone is in the market for a beachcomber. I work cheap.

My dad's the best. I love him so much!

CHAPTER THREE (FROM LEE MCPHERSON'S POV): "Bird and Yurt Life"

I still find great joy in entering the only entrance, through a bright red wooden door, to our yurt---I had cleared the seven stairs to the small circular deck we'd recently built around it in an energetic leap. *No big deal*, I tell myself as my legs are long, so I have fun using them. Even though I'm super tall for my age, I may stoop more than I have to in entering under the head jamb. I was told by a psychiatrist, who my father and I went to after my mom ditched us for drugs, that the stooping is a self-esteem issue, but I think it's because I don't want to hit my head on the top part of the framework. I quickly scan the inside of our cozy home to see if my father is here or outside. If he's inside this time of day, he's usually lounging in the ultra comfy pleather chair with ottoman. We picked it up at Goodwill for a great price recently, so he's often here watching our 40" television. Our television isn't a flat screen, but my father got it for a fairly good price from a woman named Jo who no longer needed it, as she'd just bought a 100" flatscreen to watch her beloved football games on. She works with my dad at Lucas Shipment (a Southeastern delivery company). Dad feels lucky to have the job.

Since there's only one really big room in our yurt of about 730 square feet, I'd have seen my father right away if he'd been inside.

I look at this as an opportunity to dig 'it' out of the fake bottom I'd discovered in my hamper. Well, not so much of a fake bottom by design, as we'd bought it second-hand, and it was starting to come apart at the bottom, so I reinforced it with a foursquare board I'd bought at the Habitat for Humanity Homestore, and I discovered in doing so that I had a small space between the original bottom which I left there and the new board of wood. So, I store 'it' there. I fetch it, careful to watch the door in case my father suddenly walks in. I do NOT want him seeing me with 'it.'

The Chanel scarf feels so good against my cheek, and I swear I can almost smell the fragrance she wore every night tucking me in. Chanel's 'Chance.' There's no way it would still be scented after all these years, but maybe it triggers an olfactory memory? I sure hope it's not phantosmia. No big deal, so what if I have olfactory hallucinations?! If I do, then I surely won't be sharing the information with anyone. Not sure exactly why, but her scarf still comforts me for some strange reason, though I don't want to bring my father anymore pain by seeing me with it and perhaps triggering a painful memory of her in *his* head.

We'd had it really rough when she left us. Yet, I know she thought she was doing the right thing due to her heroin addiction. Still…we lost our house because my father couldn't afford to make the mortgage payments on his own, so we left Upstate New York to come down South for my father's new job (and where the cost of living was supposed to be less expensive). We were living in Downtown Charleston in a rental which was NOT inexpensive (my father could have done better research on the area but his mind wasn't exactly right after my mother left and he was hasty to leave Upstate New York because it reminded him of her). Even though I'm sure I remind my father of her, I'm glad he took me, I smile grimly. Facing the dark thoughts sometimes makes them dissipate, I have learned. Don't think my father gets that quite yet, I muse. However, my father also mustered enough internal strength to take George and Marjorie as well, and they must remind him of her, too. George and Marjorie are our homing pigeons. They are family, so I'm so happy he did the right thing in bringing them with us! He and my mom used to have many homing pigeons as pets because it reminded them of the photo shoot they were both modelling in when they met. Hard to believe my father used to be young and good-looking enough to model with his care and weather-worn face now. Though when he smiles, I can almost see it. He doesn't smile often enough. The latter part of his life has taken its toll on him. Bringing myself back to the pigeons mentally, I love that we have George and Marjorie with us still!

My father's job fell through the first month we moved down here, and we became homeless when an unsympathetic landlord evicted us. We were homeless for about 6 months. We lived under the Cooper River Bridge. We were still in Downtown Charleston technically, but in a much more dangerous location---both weather-wise (we were exposed to the elements with no walls around us besides a cheap tent we bought) and people-wise (we had to watch out for thieves constantly). George and Marjorie even lived with us when we lived under the Cooper River Bridge. They may have helped keep us safe as pretty sure many of the thieves thought we were too crazy to mess with that much. It was rough!

Shaking myself from my *reverie* with a *no big deal*, I carefully put back my mother's scarf in its hiding place and bound outside to find my father.

I walked the rugged path and in a few minutes I was in front of George and Marjorie's aviary. We'd adopted two friends for them we'd met while living under the Cooper River Bridge: Setra and Jetavi. Setra and Jetavi are also pigeons, but they're a different kind. They're rock pigeons, and they're found throughout many parts of Downtown Charleston. Setra was injured when I saved her. I witnessed a cruel human piece of shit, who was living under the bridge with us, hit her with a large rock for no good reason. He merely said, filthy bird, as an excuse. The heartless man had aimed for Setra's head, but fortunately he'd only hit her wing. However, Setra was having difficulty getting around afterwards, and her mate (many pigeons bond with the same mate for life), Jetavi, was understandably distressed as a result. I told my father what I'd seen, and he told me to see if I could round up Setra and Jetavi (we gave them their names after two pigeons my father'd bonded with years ago in Upstate New York). He said if they got along alright with Marjorie and George, then we'd keep them and nurse

Setra back to health. It was like Setra and Jetavi knew I was there to help them when I gathered them and brought them to our meager home, the tent, under the bridge. And, George and Marjorie took to them as well.

Back to today, it looked like my father had already cleaned up the aviary housing George, Marjorie, Setra and Jetavi. I found him busy cleaning the second one, for our bird family doesn't end with the four already mentioned. My father and I took a lot of pride in having recently completed our building of the second aviary. And, it doesn't house pigeons of any breed. No, it is the home of the latest additions to our family: peace eagles (otherwise known as turkey vultures). We only have two peace eagles in the second aviary. Like Setra, we found them injured. But not under the Cooper River Bridge. Rather, we found them here in the woods of Edisto. We think they'll get along with our pigeons, but to be on the safe side, we keep them, Philyra and Demisi, separated for now.

My father is busy cleaning one of the sheltered corners of the newer aviary for Philyra and Demisi. There are two cute shelter boxes we'd built in their 12 feet (long) by 12 feet (high) home. The shelter boxes are to protect them even further inside---from the sun and rain. The screened in outer structure protects them from predators. George, Marjorie, Setra and Jetavi's aviary is about twice as big since there are twice as many of them.

See you're taking it easy, I grin and say with good-hearted sarcasm, as my father has worked up a good sweat from all the cleaning.

You betcha. Turns out, Christians aren't the only ones who believe in not having 'idle hands.' Well, he pauses and winks at me, I believe in that and no trite phrases as a general rule.

I love it when he lightens up enough to joke, as we definitely stand out in Charleston and Edisto for being decidedly Atheist.

Not even Agnostic. It is different for sure around these parts. Add to that our being vegetarians. Plus, my dad's sense of humour which is anything but mundane. Yep, I suppose we're a triple threat to some.

By the way, I'm doing great, thanks for asking, he jokes again, playing off of my initial greeting to him. Except, he pauses, I had one of those damn nightmares again last night. I watch his countenance change from one of ease to one of dread right before my eyes as he purses his lips and sucks in his breath.

Yikes, the one where the zombies rise and our infrastructure is destroyed within weeks? I ask.

Yep, except for this time ground zero is right here in Edisto. The zombies come from the ocean. And, there are different kinds of zombies.

At that, I smile. That's kinda more improbable. Different kinds of zombies? What…would some qualify to be in Mensa International? I look at him with a smartass lopsided smile. I continue with, And, the outbreak generally starts in New

York in your nightmares. I mean, with New York City being so heavily populated, an undead infestation starting and spreading there makes more sense. I don't tell my father that I feel some relief flood over me, as that old nightmare of his upset me because my mother is probably still in New York. Neither of his 'nightmare scenarios' are ideal, however, as we're obviously here still.

Let's just hope both scenarios remain just that: nightmares, my father volunteers. Now, help me finish cleaning this for Philyra and Demisi.

At that Philyra, brings me a thick piece of rope she likes to play with, cocks her red head to the side and says in her peace eagle way: Play with me. She likes to engage in a kind of tug of war with me gently. I love her so much…and, all our feathered friends!

CHAPTER 3: (FROM RELIABLE [SO SHE TELLS ME] NARRATOR'S POV) "Sides Taken"

The next day at school is already off to a crappy start for Luis, Mr. Mehia and Lee. Mr. Mehia fell earlier that morning, when his post-op knee locked up unexpectedly on him as he was hurrying down the stairs to make Luis breakfast. As a result, Mr. Mehia and Luis were late in leaving their beachfront house to pick up Lee in the country. He joked to his son that he couldn't be held responsible for always staying vertical. However, Luis knew his dad was scared, as he'd fallen down about 7 stairs and had been speaking to him in 'Spanglish' which was a sure sign he was rattled (figuratively and literally). He'd beseeched Luis with, por favor, mijo, no doing eso (when Luis had wanted to call 911).

ECHS (Edisto Cusabo High School) is about 20 minutes from the McPherson's yurt on a normal day, but today Mother Nature is in a bad mood. It is Hurricane Season, so not too surprising, and some branches from oak trees have fallen on South Carolina Highway 174 on our way to ECHS. SC 174 is a National Scenic Byway, and normally it's a pleasure riding to ECHS because of the view, but not today. In fact, the news channels have been covering a tropical storm for a few days, but most South Carolinians are fairly calm unless the storm changes into a Category 3 or higher hurricane. The meteorologists are thinking that the tropical storm will gather force and speed throughout the day to become a Category 1, but around these parts, a Category 1 Hurricane doesn't even close down schools. Obviously, as Luis and Lee are walking to their lockers next to each other within minutes of waving goodbye to Mr. Mehia.

Lee is holding out hope that the day may still be salvaged from 'suckdom'…that is, until he goes to open his locker, and it's immediately slammed shut by the resident bully: Mel Rene Paltry

Punk suuucks, Mel drawls, offering his unsolicited advice, while looking up at Lee in his black TSOL t-shirt, even though Lee was slouching (yep, Mel's short as fuck), as he manages to push Lee up against his now closed locker because Lee isn't fighting back. What Mel severely lacks in height, he's maybe 5 foot 2 inches when wearing shoes with more of a heel, he makes up for in girth. His family calls it theek-sayit. Many people would write it thickset and pronounce it quite differently.

Easy man, Luis commands, giving Mel a title he's not worthy of to diffuse the situation.

Standin' up fer yer buoy-friend? Mel taunts.

Not daunted, Luis replies, thinking of beautiful Graciela, And, if I were? Would your bigoted-self have a problem with that?

At that, Mel closes his shit-brown colored eyes, which many had commented on as looking chillingly dead as well, and he backs up a bit. It was well known around school that Luis was well-trained in some martial arts, namely aikido, jujitsu and Jeet Kune Do, and he had won several competitions years ago. He stopped competing after his mother's death and when surfing kind of took its place. The fact that he was super fluid in his martial arts movements in the past probably aided him in being a great surfer at this point as well.

Trying desperately to save face, Mel's unappealing visage turns red to the roots of his thinning shit-brown colored hair. Coward that he is, he merely mumbles with his paper-thin lips, Go ate yer faggie vegetarrian lunch tuhgether thane. After speaking his dull mind, Mel shambles off to find someone to pick on who has no friends. Having no luck with that, he congregates with a group of his bullying friends: Connor Cravaho (whose mother is rumored to be a Black Widow Killer with two husbands dying under suspicious circumstances in less than five years), Dottie Asseley (a criminal who is already blackmailing family members at 16-years old), et cetera.

Even if Mel weren't mumbling, not all would understand him, Lee thinks with an inward smile. Gotta love it when a bully like Mel is foiled, he inner-dialogues more.

Mel's bad behavior was noticed by a group of concerned 'upstanders' (those who will stand up to bullies on behalf of those being belittled). One of them in particular, a slender and gracefully tall Goth girl named Gianna, who Lee *notices* regularly himself.

Mundanes, whatcha gonna do?! Gianna quips with a smile, looking at Lee when Mel is out of earshot.

Lee immediately smiles back at her. Nothing, that's what. 'Cause I don't think a mugshot would capture my face at its best angle.

Definitely not worth doing time for some shady asshole, Gianna continues.

They take shady to a new level. He and his uncle. More like they're into schadenfreude, Lee whispers, wary of such an accusation at the school where Mel's uncle happens to be the principal.

Gianna beams at Lee's non-mundane word choice. She leans in to whisper to him, *No worries, my intelligent friend, as I doubt they'd understand what schadenfreude means even if they heard it. And, I've never seen them looking up words for clarity on Google either.*

Lee feels much better. A dose of Gianna's grey matter always does that to him.

Then, a cute petite girl walks up to Luis and touches his elbow gently offering, Brave of you sticking up for your friend like that. She looks up at him with admiration, catching her breath a bit looking into his intense midnight blue eyes. While Luis in turn finds himself flushing a bit. She has that effect on him. Even with the four-inch heels she's wearing, she barely comes up to Luis's shoulder, and Luis finds that super appealing. In fact, there's not a thing about Graciela that he doesn't find appealing.

Yeah, I don't tolerate the bully thing on my watch, Luis responds.

All upstanders' watch, Graciela muses, thinking of the heteronormative codes she has to deal with daily being transgender.

CHAPTER 4: (FROM NARRATOR'S POV) "Hurricane Willa"

The rest of the school day at ECHS is passing by uneventfully, at least for now, except for those following the news on their smartphones are seeing that meteorologists are talking, without much alarm, about the tropical storm which has now turned into a Category 1 Hurricane. Her name is Hurricane Willa, and she's already pounding parts of the South Carolina coastline with heavy winds and rain.

Far more interesting, perhaps, than anything going on at ECHS, at the moment, is what's been stewing under the pier that Renah Lousquat Conoher is standing on. Renah's restaurant, Smythe's, is on the beachfront about 20 miles from ECHS. Desperate to get a smoke in, despite Hurricane Willa's winds, somewhat oblivious Renah Lousquat Conoher is standing on the pier puffing away on her vape pen (the kind with nicotine liquid). Edisto no longer allows smoking of any kind in eating establishments, so addict that she is, she will go outside to smoke in any weather. It's just her and a fisherman on the pier. He waves hello to Renah with a toothless grin. Hope I'll have some fish for you shortly. Hurricanes generally make for good fishing!

Renah loves boasting her restaurant generally serves fresh fish for their signature fish and chips: Smythe's Fish & Chips. She says it's to serve the people the best, but it's really because getting her fish from the toothless fisherman, Mystilo, is a lot less expensive for her since his fish are never regulated. Plus, unless she gets the fish from Mystilo, it's the frozen kind she buys in the grocery store. So, her saying *generally* isn't accurate.

The years have not been kind to Renah who aids their unkindess by being a chain smoker. First cigarettes and now vapes. Delusional, she thinks vaping is much better for her, but she's still inhaling nicotine. Her vaping now is, however, much better for Mother Earth, as she no longer throws her cigarette butts on the ground. With smoker's lips, a poor diet (heavy in meat-laden meals and too much alcohol) and not much exercise, she is a 45 year old who looks 65 (and that's being generous).

A betting person might say Renah could easily be dead (from a heart attack or something else she could have prevented) within the next five years easily. Yet, what's stirring in the Atlantic Ocean below her feet could not be predicted: it's a recipe not in Mother Nature's cookbook, as it's too new…while at the same time ancient.

Renah is lulled to further laziness by the waves moving about 75 feet beneath where she's standing on the pier to lap up against the honey-colored sand on the shore. About 150 feet from the shoreline is Smythe's. Renah doesn't care about Hurricane Willa except for wanting no mandatory closings of businesses later on. What she lacks in desire for personal physical upkeep, she makes up for in what she considers more important: chasing the almighty dollar. Prone to laziness physically, that 'chase' is the only exercise Renah's into.

What's been brewing beneath Renah's feet began 15 million years ago, for it was then that a bright yellowish brown tektite-like glass meteoroid, about the size of cherry, splashed into the Atlantic Ocean---not far from where Smythe's was built millions of years later. This meteoroid became buried under the ocean floor over time. Yet, with all the hurricane activity growing in recent years, it had been gradually dislodging from its long-held stable resting spot. Though only a Category 1, Hurricane Willa made sure it completely freed today!

The bright topaz-looking meteoroid's freedom is short-lived as it catches the indiscrimination of a smaller-size lancet fish's voracious appetite. Known for their cannibalism as well, the lancet fish is not picky in food choices to satisfy their incredible hunger.

At the same time Renah enters her restaurant through the back door (which leads right into the kitchen), with its peeling rust-colored paint around the frame and a torn screen, Mystilo is whistling through his nonexistent teeth at having caught the lancet fish. Unusual to find one in this area, he thinks, but he's heard their meat is sweet. Smiling at the prospect of pocketing a few extra bucks today, he heads towards Smythe's back door with the unlucky lancet fish.

Renah's place is generally filled with her regulars who frequent Smythe's for a late lunch. Knowing she couldn't compete with other lunchtime restaurants with the big 'C Rating' (for food safety) on her door, she decided a few years ago to offer a late lunch special when many restaurants were closed (after their lunch crowds) to clean up before their dinner crowds. That way Renah didn't need to worry about ever striving for an A or B rating since she would always have business without having to have a super clean place.

Today was different, though, as the hurricane was probably keeping many away from Smythe's. Wimps, Renah thinks. Afraid of a Category 1 Hurricane. Ridiculous, she continues thinking, with disgust.

CHAPTER 5: (FROM NARRATOR'S POV) "Mega-Smiting at Smythe's"

The only waiter working at Smythe's (located about five minutes by car from Mr. Mehia's beachfront place and 15 minutes if walking) is an imbecilic one named Evan Scourga. He considers himself better than menial labor, but his anti-Mason occult social media sites don't pay the bills. In reality, he's a perfect fit for Smythe's workforce. Renah rings the call bell from behind the sprawling, weathered bar with cigarette burns in the shellacked cheap wood. Sea shells had been erratically glued on the wood before the varnish had been applied. Depressingly, it seemed like the shells were drowning in the shellac covering them, some more deeply than others. One or two shells have almost achieved freedom from the bar, as part of them is jutting out, into the unvarnished world. The bar separates the front section of the restaurant from the back. It doesn't take Renah long to bake the strange-smelling lancet fish she bought for next to nothing from Mystilo. She figured the weird smell was typical for the lancet fish, as she didn't usually prepare it. She saves some of the fish after frying it for herself and Evan. Evan always eats at Smythe's since his food is half off.

Evan sets the order of lancet fish and greasy chips in front of a regular: Lizzie Jado. Barely looking up from the four-seater table (she always sits at it selfishly, regardless of how crowded it is, in order to spread out whatever she's working on), as she's engrossed in tearing off the plastic wrap, which she carelessly lets fall to the floor and stay there, to a new deck of tarot cards. Then, she begins to pick at the fish. She's slender and enjoys the attention she gets from her 'thin privilege,' so she only ingests a small portion of food generally---as in, only a bite here and a bite there actually being swallowed. However, with her new tarot deck before her, she feels like she needs more 'brain food' today, so she starts to eat the fish quickly, barely stopping to chew each bite. Pretty much straight to her gullet it goes before starting to gather maliciously in her stomach.

Since it is so slow, with Lizzie as his only customer, Renah lets Evan sit down between serving her to eat his own lunch of the lancet fish and chips. He's a voracious eater, and he stares with sideways glances at Lizzie the entire time he's eating, as if he'd like to devour her, too. With her new tarot deck out, Evan feels even closer to Lizzie. She represents the feminine energy of his mother, he feels. He hates his father's masculine energy which he erroneously connotes with all Masons. Even more creepy is the fact that Lizzie reminds him of his mother, and he has an arguably strange attraction to both.

Evan is sitting at the bar across from Renah, sideways in his chair, so he can check out Lizzie while being attentive to his duties as a waiter. He follows Renah's orders religiously, much as he did his own mother's. Renah is also taking a break now to eat her fish and chips.

However, Renah's interrupted soon after by Joey, a heavy-set trucker in his mid-thirties, stopping in to place an order. Joey's order makes the last of the ill-fated lancet fish which has now fed three horrid humans and will feed him later on. Joey gets his order to go.

Thawing out the frozen grocery-bought fish now, after making sure Joey left with his order sealed tightly as he doesn't plan on eating it till he drops off his shipment in Winston-Salem, NC (about two hours from Edisto the way he speeds), Renah then gets back to eating what's left of her special Smythe's Fish & Chips meal.

Mystilo was right, Renah thinks, the lancet fish does taste sweet. Looking across at Evan enjoying his fish, too, she thinks it's strange he's starting to sweat profusely. Suddenly, she feels flushed and starts sweating, too. Looking at Lizzie, she sees sweat dripping profusely on the top cards of her tarot deck: the Tower and the Death cards eerily saturated. Renah tries to ask them if they're alright before she blacks out. Her last thought was thinking how strange it is that they're so hot since the old air conditioning unit and large dusty ceiling fan are both still working just fine.

20 minutes later, Mystilo knocks on the back entrance door with his fishing pole and fish bucket in tow. He's caught more fish! Looking to make a few more bucks that day, he keeps knocking, expecting to see Renah open the door any minute. But, she doesn't. Emboldened by the prospect of making more money than usual and eager to have a break from the hurricane force winds and rain, Mystilo enters through the back door to the kitchen. It groans with age and disrepair. Mystilo shakes his head as the door almost sounds like it's saying, Gooooo foool.

He sees the store-bought fish first, nearly thawed now by the fish fryer. Chips are frying in shallow oil unattended. He approaches the kitchen-side of the bar where he sees Renah slumped over the bar before him. Strange time to take a siesta, he ponders, as his stomach begins to knot with inexplicable dread.

Mystilo sees Evan next, across the bar from Renah, sleeping. He can't see either of their faces. However, he's chilled to the bone when he sees a pretty woman with lifeless eyes and drool coming from the corner of her mouth awake at her table. It's Lizzie…she is looking directly at him now. Her mouth agape, she rises slowly from her chair. She shambles towards Mystilo. As Lizzie had eaten the tainted fish first, she changed first.

Mystilo doesn't know exactly what's happening, but he's watched enough zombie flicks to know not to stick around and find out. Smart move, as Evan is starting to stir. Grateful for the bar separating what he perceives as 'Shambler Lizzie' from him, Mystilo intends to make his exit quickly through the kitchen, the way he came in. So, Mystilo turns abruptly, but his fishing pole's hook is caught in the process on one of the shells half-way freed from the shellac. It's as if the shell's trying to use the hook to free itself completely from the prison of Smythe's.

The problem shell is to the right of where Renah's slumped over at the bar.

Mystilo won't leave his fishing pole, as it's his livelihood. Desperately trying to free it from the shell, he moves to the right of Renah and bends over to get a better look. Whistling through his gums, he is amazed at how stuck the hook is. More stuck than in any poor fish who'd had to endure the hook's brutal metal only to be captured and eaten. Working on freeing his hook further, Mystilo bends over even more, so he doesn't notice Renah stirring to the left of him till it's too late. She takes a big chunk out of his left arm before he realizes that his livelihood is not as important as his life.

So, Mystilo bends his right arm up quickly to forcefully bring it down to break his own rod in half. It works. The hook remains stuck in the shell along with the tip and part of the mid-section of the pole. However, the handle, reel and the other part of the mid-section have just become a repurposed weapon for him. Wasting no time, Mystilo determinedly uses his new weapon to drive it into Renah's already decomposing temple.

Whistling again through no teeth, Mystilo marvels at this sort of zombie. Like nothing he's seen in the movies. In the movies he's seen, there's no rapid decomposition like this. She's a shambler…he begins thinking. No…no…that's not it…decomp's more like it, he mutters to himself.

There is barely time to let the term he coined sink in before Decomp Lizzie, who had shambled up to a now reanimated Decomp Evan at the bar, and Decomp Evan both lung at the bar (separating them from Mystilo) to get at the sweet meal they smell in him. They don't just want Mystilo's brains; they want to devour him literally from head to toe.

Mystilo smiles at their sloshy ineptness, as he reaches over the bar to drive his weaponized rod into Evan's temple. Evan falls to the floor with a wet thud, as his membrane has thinned to bursting in his rapidly decomposing state. A large quantity of Decomp Evan's blood, now a black-red color, is pooling on the floor. Klutzy Decomp Lizzie slips in it. As she tries to get up, Mystilo jumps over the bar with his weaponized rod and sinks it into her temple.

Mystilo finally has the opportunity to look down at his left arm. The bite mark is becoming more pronounced. He's seen enough zombie flicks to know that there's a good chance he's in real trouble. He can't let anyone know he's been bitten, or he could be killed like he'd just killed three decomps. Then it occurs to him…like soothing waves lapping up against the shore…he'll go into the ocean. Salt water won't cure the type of zombie (a decomp) that he is, but he doesn't know that. And, hurricane winds don't scare him, so he tries to jump back over the bar to make his way out the back door and leave the bloodbath behind him. Yet, he's thwarted, as he suddenly starts sweating profusely…and he's so dizzy that he can't jump back over the bar…maybe he can just rest his head for a few minutes on the bar first and then get in the ocean, he thinks sluggishly and futilely…

CHAPTER 6: (FROM NARRATOR'S POV, IN MOSTLY JO'S JARGON) "Mr. Mehia's Unexpected Memento Mori"

Jo, a butch woman in her late 30s, is cursing in her delivery truck. She hates her job, but she strives to be punctual nonetheless. She was late in picking up her boxes from LS (Lucas Shipment, a parcel delivery company she's worked for about a year), so she was late in taking lunch. It was the first time she'd allowed her whiney girlfriend to make her late, and she was annoyed at that. Yep, placing the blame was easy: It all started earlier that morning when her needy femme girlfriend, Jennifer Chiste, started freaking out on her about some whack nightmare she'd had where the dead rose again. As Jo knows Jennifer suffers from neurosis, Jo takes Jennifer's hysteria with a grain of salt. Still, it took some time to calm her back down. Jo was about to put on her short-sleeved cotton/polyester blend work shirt, that she'd applied her last name Baumerde to over the left pocket, over her sports bra when she was interrupted by Jennifer freaking out. Jo had to stop her morning routine to go and comfort Jennifer with hugs and lots of soothing words like, it'll be alright, baby. Jennifer didn't work. She lived off of the tax payer's dime in collecting social security, and she wasn't the most respectful of others' work schedules because she didn't have one of her own. Having coddled Jennifer extensively this particular morning, even more than normal, made Jo late for work. Then came Hurricane Willa which set Jo even further behind schedule.

Jo didn't like getting food from a restaurant with just a C Rating, but the other restaurants on her route were already closed to open again later for their dinner crowds. At least the place Jo pulls her truck up to offer their food to go, as she hopes to scarf down the food before her next delivery. She doesn't have time to take a sit-down lunch, as she has to make up time she'd lost earlier. She feels like she needs some heavy-duty grub, like a big greasy burger with fries, before the next dropoff, as the dude receiving the shipment is to get 10 heavy boxes which she'd loaded earlier. He lives about five minutes from the dilapidated eatery. She hopes the place has red meat and not just seafood.

An overpowering stench assaults Jo's nostrils when she opens the front door to Smythe's. Damn, not sure I wanna eat here, she says aloud, but under her breath. Taking inventory of the restaurant, only looking eye and chair level, she doesn't see the doubly-dead former staff, et cetera on the floor in pools of their own now partially-congealed blood. Instead, she only sees some bum asleep at the bar with a mangled fishing rod beside him.

Jo decides to walk up to the bar to see if she can get some service. Big mistake! At first she thinks it's a joke. Some employee shenanigans. Then she wonders if there's a zombie flick or something being shot there. Then she realizes that the real life foul smell isn't being faked. Oh my gawd! she shouts like a femme, then composes herself the next moment as is the butch way. At her shout, the 'bum' at the bar, Decomp Mystilo, raises his head. Now he's standing and looking at Jo with lifeless eyes. Then he lunges for her, his now white fingernails sink deeply into her arms, as he hopes to pull himself closer to her for a bite of any of her flesh he can get. Decomp Mystilo's taller than Jo, but he'd been sitting, so they're both at about the same head level. Snapping herself out of disbelief, Jo realizes that she needs to fight for her life, and she remembers the disfigured fishing pole she'd seen. Strangely enough, it's Mystilo's own pole that causes his second death, as she grabs it and pushes it with force between Decomp Mystilo's dead eyes. She wasn't one to lose a fight with a dude, be they dead or alive.

Looking down at her arms, she sees the gashes in them that the zombie Mystilo made. Heading to her truck, she finds it slightly amusing that she'll be using the first aid kit (mandatory that all delivery drivers equip their trucks with it) she never thought she'd have to use. In her truck, she douses her arms with hydrogen peroxide, and bandages them quickly. Patting her Buddha belly, she attempts some humor with, Well, at least I'll be losing some weight today with no lunch and more physical activity than I counted on. Even though she never mentioned it to Jennifer, it scared her that she would be as big as her one day. Jo wasn't as much of a feminist as she fooled herself into thinking, for she found herself thinking about being with a more aesthetically pleasing to her (AKA a slender femme) frequently.

Mr. Mehia is tidying up his foyer a bit before his company arrives. John is a friend from Mount Pleasant who is going to the monthly vegetarian meetup soon. He is still a pescatarian, so he isn't a vegetarian yet, but he's already given up red meat. It's a start. As their vegetarian meetup allows those who are curious about going vegetarian and vegan as well, John is allowed to attend. Also, it is nice that John has volunteered to hand out fliers (recyclable), which Mr. Mehia already has ready on his marble entryway table.

John said he'll hand them out at his work in Mount Pleasant for the monthly event. Super nice considering he's travelling all the way from Mount Pleasant to Mr. Mehia's place in Edisto.

As Mr. Mehia is also expecting a big shipment of memento mori, he walks into the kitchen looking for box cutters in one of his drawers. His doorbell rings. Damn, he mutters. These'll have to do, he thinks, grabbing a large pair of scissors.

Placing the scissors on top of the fliers on the same ornate, for a beach house, marble top table in the foyer, Carlos Mehia opens the door. It's John. Closing the door behind him, John enters the foyer.

Good to see you, Carlos. Hey, I saw an LS truck in your driveway. Need my help in unloading anything? I saw the driver unloading a lot of boxes onto her dolly. I thought about asking her if she needed any help as she was sweating profusely. John knows that Carlos is impaired still due to his fairly recent knee surgery, as his gait is still off.

They both were startled the next second, for an inexplicable reason, at hearing the doorbell ring. Call it an ominous foreboding, but both Carlos and John feel it. Being closest to the door, John opens it, trying to shake off the feeling of dread, as he figures it's probably just the deliverywoman from Lucas Shipment.

And, it is. Sort of. With mouth already agape in expectation of a meal from the yummy smelling seafood-eater (John), Decomp Jo lunges for him and sinks her teeth into his right arm. What the hell? John starts, trying to push the short creature off of him. In her Decomp state, Jo's unrelentingly forceful, and she knocks John to the ground where she manages to crawl on top of him and bite the right side of his neck as well.

Que jodienda, girlia (Spanglish cross between girl and chica)! Trying to pull Decomp Jo off of his friend to no avail with his limited mobility thanks to his recovering knee, Carlos reaches for the scissors he was going to use to open his boxes of memento mori and plunges them into Decomp Jo's left temple instead. Being a purveyor of memento mori he remembers that all have to die…even if it's twice, he thinks grimly.

CHAPTER 7: (FROM NARRATOR'S POV) "Inhospitality at the Hospital and ECHS"

Grabbing the vegetarian meetup fliers next, Carlos places some of the fliers on the already festering wound on his friend's neck and some on the already festering wound on his arm.

Get me to the hospital, John pleads. Carlos knows that calling and waiting for an ambulance will take more time than if he just drives his friend there. Grimball Hospital is 20 minutes from the Mehia's place, so he grabs his keys and carries John in a limping fireman's carry to his Bugatti Veyron. Quite a Herculean effort, as Carlos' knee is not the most reliable. Thankfully, it didn't pick then to lock on him. And, as taking care of his friend trumps ruining his custom-made pleather interior, he somehow manages to lay his bleeding friend in the back seat.

Speeding from his beachfront home to get to the hospital, he calls his friend Thomas McPherson about picking up their sons at school, as he's obviously dealing with an emergency situation.

Thomas answers the phone in his LS truck. He's just pulling up to the yurt. He needs to check on the birds with Hurricane Willa in force. Hi, Carlos. What's up, my friend?

It's…it's Juan…I mean, John. He's been hurt. I'm taking him to the hospital. Can you pick up the boys?

Sure. And, I'll swing by the hospital with the boys afterwards. What happened?

Too much to explain right now, and I'm not even sure I understand myself. Just be careful, and watch the boys.

Of course! Thomas answered apprehensively. We'll see you after I pick them up then.

Thomas hurriedly leaves his truck to check on the birds. A branch has fallen on the roof of the aviary housing George and Marjorie, the homing pigeons. Showing his concern by sucking in his breath and puckering his lips, Thomas's heart skips a beat when he sees that another branch has torn the screen on the right side. Thomas doesn't know what he'll do if George and Marjorie aren't alright. They're feathered family!! He walks into their aviary and looks around. His homing pigeons are nowhere to be found! However, Setra and Jetavi are still there…in the damaged aviary. They're huddled together fearfully.

Gulping, he looks at the second aviary. Philyra and Demisi are there, and their aviary has sustained no damage from Hurricane Willa. Philyra hops towards Thomas and cocks her head to the side looking at him intently as if to say, I wish I could tell you what happened. She then looks at Setra and Jetavi as if to say: It's fine, you can put them here with us. They're family!

Well, I've been thinking you'll all get along anyway, so here goes, Thomas says aloud, as he transfers a shaken Setra and Jetavi into Philyra and Demisi's aviary. Within seconds, Philyra hops over to Setra with her head cocked to the side to say, Welcome!

Seeing with relief that Hurricane Willa's winds are also dying down, Thomas heads to pick up the boys from ECHS. He'll be picking them up a bit early. He's sure the school will understand an emergency situation. Then, it'll be on to Grimball Hospital, with the boys to find Carlos and John, which is just a five minute drive from ECHS.

Thomas has no idea how he'll break the news to Lee that George and Marjorie have literally flown the coup.

• •

Carlos drives up to the emergency room entrance of the Grimball Hospital. Even though Carlos made the normally 20 minutes' drive from his house to the hospital in record time (about 14 minutes), his friend John had slipped into unconsciousness sometime along the way.

Kasey Readylaw Drope has been principal at ECHS for too long. His culturally backwards ways keep the private school from moving forward into this century in many ways. The labs inhumanely still use real frogs (instead of computer simulation), etc. for dissection for starters, and his English department is pathetic. As Principal Drope doesn't use proper English himself, he doesn't see why English is a subject that should be stressed. Plus, the foreign language department is also lacking with only two languages offered: French and Spanish. The Theatre Department is almost nonexistent, except for the annual Christmas Play (which leaves out other religions and Atheists, obviously).

Principal Drope is ironically 'unprincipled.' And, quite unhealthy. He eats far too many processed foods, except for the poor animals he kills in illegal canned hunting events. They are fresh meat. His favorite being venison, and the younger the deer, the tastier to him. He had no problem in killing and eating beautiful fawns.

Even though his doctor has warned of heart disease down the road for him, Principal Drope stubbornly hasn't changed his eating habits. To the detriment of his health and more importantly to the detriment of the health of the poor fawns he kills regularly to feed his gluttonous appetite.

Principal Drope has been experiencing chest pains all day, and Hurricane Willa hadn't been helping matters. Then, his dopey nephew, Mel Paltry, comes by his office and sits down to complain of unfair treatment by Lee, Luis, et cetera, even though Mel had been the one stirring the shit pot. As Principal Drope doesn't want to hear his sister's complaining at their Baptist church on Sunday about how unfairly her son, Mel, is being treated in school, he decides he's going to give detention to all of them: Lee, Luis, Mel, Gianna and Graciela. That way Principal Drope is covering his own ass, not caring in the least about what's fair. First, grinning from ear to ear, as he's about to dismiss Mel and call his secretary in to handle all the details of the detention, after his what he takes to be his own brilliance in handling the situation via his venal verdict, Principal Drope's face then rapidly changes to one of fearful shock as he experiences a massive heart attack. Seeing his uncle slump into his chair unconscious, Mel stands up and shuffles to his uncle's desk to call 911. Hey, this here's Mel...mah uuncle's hade a hart attacke I thank.

■■■

Lou Medico had become a paramedic about 15 years ago, and he was a good one. He was capable and calm in emergency situations, and most people he treated appreciated that. The fact that he got tired of waiting on his inheritance, so he was prompted to become one, doesn't change the fact that he has wonderful life-saving skills. His mother had given him quite a bit of money over the years anyway, but he had yet to receive the mother lode, so to speak. So, he often took on extra shifts at Grimball Hospital (he primarily worked for Roper Hospital in Charleston) to bolster his bank account. Lou finishes the last of his foot-long meatball sub, careful to check his teeth for any leftover food, and gets out at GH to soon start his shift. A man in a Bugatti Veyron is struggling with something in his back seat. It's an unconscious man. Carlos Mehia sees Lou Medico approaching and desperately asks, Please…you work here…por favor, ayudame?

Lou thinks about waiting for a gurney since he isn't on the clock yet, but then he thinks of the praise (and maybe a raise) he'll receive for helping out before his shift has even started. So, he reaches in to help get the stirring to consciousness now Decomp John out. Decomp John is aware of one arm smelling delicious (meat-eater Lou's) and one being not at all desirable (vegetarian Carlos's). Decomp John lunges forward to try and take a bite out of Lou's hairy arm when Carlos sees the situation and manages, even with his wonky knee, to push John back on the seat. Carlos remembers all too well what Decomp Jo did to John.

Please, he's sick. I don't know what he's afflicted with, but he's dangerous. Can you bring out a sedative of some sort…make it fuerto..fuertong…I mean, strong…make it a strong one! Carlos looks behind his back for a moment to see the situation people-wise, as he doesn't want Decomp John to lunge at anyone else. Thankfully, the coast is clear, except in the moment Carlos turns around, Decomp John tries to pull himself up off the seat where Carlos had pushed him by using Lou's right arm. Decomp John's sickly fingernails scratch him. Thinking nothing of it, Lou simply rolls his sleeve down over the scratches. He's had tripped out drug addicts inflict worse wounds on his body, or so he thinks.

Carlos didn't see what had just transpired, as Lou had pushed Decomp John back down on the seat by the time he turned back around, so Lou starts walking into the ER next with, I'll send someone out with a sedative.

Hurry! Carlos emphasizes, as he locks Decomp John in his car.

Carlos is surprised to see a different paramedic approach him in a few minutes. Right after clocking in, Lou had been called to ECHS…a man there has had a heart attack.

∎∎

Having no idea how close they all were to getting detention, Lee, Gianna, Luis and Graciela are talking by their lockers after their last classes for the day. Lee can't get enough of Gianna's symphonic voice: deep for a girl and powerful. Plus, she always brings interesting conversation to the table. She's been talking about taking a cryptocurrency course online, as there's nothing that cutting edge offered at ECHS. Though laughing at herself, she admits her love of watching stock market trends for bullish and bearish markets is decidedly mundane. I like to make the mundane 'fundane,' is one of Gianna's favorite made-up sayings. And, it makes her laugh even further when she considers how mundane the saying is. Lee loves Gianna's sense of humor and the idea of her taking a cryptocurrency class. If only he had money to spare to invest in Bitcoin and other Altcurrency! Gianna has him laughing aloud at her darkly delightful and silly epigram regarding old currency (the kind most people still use, she laments): AKA Fiat money. It is in tribute to her 'dime store ring' (she calls it that, but it was actually created in a rather pricey jewelry store in Downtown Charleston) with an actual dime on it. Lee can't help thinking he'd like to put a different kind of ring on her finger one day.

Gianna's poem is as follows:

I wear this dime upon my finger

So this Fiat money will still linger

As a memento mori of its death

Should have had more, eh, intrinsic worth.

She made it up on the spot when Lee complimented her ring. She wears it on her digitus secundus. She says in case she ever needs to use it as a weapon in a fight. We all smile at that, as it's a relatively small ring. She had it made with her specifications: a dime in the middle of small skulls in sterling silver. She doesn't like gold. When Luis saw it, he said it reminded him of his dad's relatively newfound memento mori style.

Gianna and Graciela have their own vehicles, but Luis and Lee don't (Luis could have one, as they've plenty of money, but he likes his dad picking him up, especially after his mother died), and Lee is too financially challenged to have one. Suddenly, an EMT, who's sweating profusely, barges through the front doors near their lockers. He's in such a hurry that he almost runs into Lee. Before Lee can process how strange that is, he's surprised to get a call from his father with, I'm picking you up today in the LS truck. Tell Luis. Mr. Mehia is at the hospital. Something's happened to John, our friend who's helping with the vegetarian meetup. We'll meet Carlos at the hospital. Luis can get a ride home from his dad then.

Surprise showing on his face, Lee looks at Luis. That was my father. He's picking us up today. Your dad is at the hospital with John, the guy interested in becoming a vegetarian.

Gianna frowns. She's felt weird energy all day and not just from Hurricane Willa's force. She can't put her finger on it, but her Gothic discernment tells her it's something morbid.

I could give you a ride, Graciela offers, touching Luis's elbow lightly.

Thanks, but I better see if my dad needs my help with John, Luis beams down at Graciela. He loves how thoughtful she is.

Totally get it, Graciela responds. I am going to get going then. These twin torture devices, she laughs, looking down at her high heels, are coming off the second I'm in my car!

All four of them are laughing at that and close their lockers almost in unison.

Lou is sweating profusely when he enters Principal Drope's office. The secretary, Debissa Eastfoul (Principal Drope is her second cousin and Mel is her first cousin once removed), asks Lou if she can get him a paper towel for his perspiration. Mel left the office to tell his sketchy friends about what had happened to his uncle after he dialed 911. Lou waves Debissa off dismissively. He's finding it difficult to think of words to say like a simple no thank you.

Shrugging, Debissa gets back to her ham sandwich. She could care less if Principal Drope lives or dies, even though he's her second cousin, as long as she keeps getting a paycheck. She's used to rudeness from Drope, who let's just say is definitely not behind the 'Me Too Movement,' so she doesn't sweat what she takes to be Lou's rudeness.

Lou sees an unconscious Drope slumped over in his once imposing but now just a cracked leather chair and sees a chair across from his (where students in trouble generally sit, where Mel, in fact, had been sitting recently). Instead of administering CPR, Lou is suddenly so exhausted that he sits in the student chair and falls into unconsciousness. Debissa is finishing the last of her meat meal when Decomp Lou awakens. Drope barely has a pulse, but that's enough for his meat-eating self to smell delicious to Decomp Lou. Decomp Lou lunges across the desk at Drope. When Debissa goes to check on Drope, she screams so shrilly that students down the hallway at their lockers come running to Drope's office. Or, at least some of them did. Mel and his cowardly posse don't want to get involved. There the brave students who decide to get involved see Decomp Lou mowing down on the left side of Drope's face…

Principal Drope likes having his office near the lockers, so he can hear conversations here and there, or at least he used to. He felt it made him a great principal. Never mind there's another not-so-great word for it: eavesdropping.

Instead of leaving school and getting into their rides, you, Dear Reader, may have guessed that brave Gianna, Lee, Luis and Graciela were the ones to run to Principal Drope's office when they heard Debissa's shriek. Debissa, not being brave, was leaving when they come rushing in. Debissa cares for the students of the school about as much as she does for Principal Drope.

Debissa flees down the school hallway. She's supposed to pick up her sister after her shift at Grimball Hospital. So what if she's a little early. She'll just sit and catch up on her favorite dating reality show. Yep, Debissa's mundane as fuck, and coward that she is, she smiles at how lucky she was to dodge the zombie bullet, so to speak.

That explains it, Gianna says aloud to her friends. The weird energy I've been feeling. Zombie energy.

Wasn't that the guy who almost ran into me near the lockers? Lee questions in a tone of disbelief. Man, he's the fasted decomposing zombie I've ever seen.

Yeah, this is nothing like in my extensive zombie movie collection. He's a different breed, Gianna continues. He should be called a Decomp. (Coincidentally, this is exactly the same term Mystilo used to describe the zombies at Smythe's.) Gianna and Lee were a bit calmer than Luis and Graciela. Gianna is a Goth, so death and an overall fascination with the macabre are in her wheelhouse. Lee, having been homeless with his father for some time, had faced harsh conditions already in his young life, so he knows how to remain level-headed in the face of adversity. Luis and Graciela not so much, though that doesn't stop them from acting bravely.

Ermagd, a z-z-ombie! Woke from the dead is the wrong kinda woke! Graciela offers in a high-pitched and shaky voice. Though Graciela is visibly and audibly upset, she tries to lighten the gravity of the situation with a joke for everyone's sake. And, even though she's brave, she leans against Luis for support.

Well, like Gianna said: A Decomp, Luis reiterates, trying to remain calm by clarifying the situation, but happy to have Graciela that close to him. He'd do anything to protect her! In the meantime, Decomp Lou continues to munch on the left side of Principal Drope's face.

When Decomp Lou gets to his eyeball, Graciela pulls it together enough to pull off one of her heels, and say, Eww…enough…we gotta stop this thing…this Decomp thingy…

CHAPTER 8: (FROM NARRATOR'S POV) "Decomps Versus Shedders"

Thomas McPherson is surprised at seeing the Principal's secretary sprinting as fast as her stocky legs can take her, out of the main school entranceway and towards her car, as he's about to enter ECHS. He shouts out to her, Is everything okay?

No, nawt reallie. Sum *thing* is in there. I've got ter go. If I was yew, then I wooed, too.

I can't go! My son and his best friend are in there! Thomas stresses.

Wha-le, yew may want ter brang somethin' ter stop *It*! a disheveled and flustered Debissa shouts, opening the door to her car and then closing it quickly and starting up the engine. She isn't staying there a second longer than she has to. She doesn't care about filling in Mr. McPherson more. She's out for herself, and she's completely forgotten that she is supposed to give her cousin Mel a ride from ECHS to Grimball Hospital, as she does every school day.

Thomas McPherson shakes his head, sucks in his breath, puckers his lips in thought and then decides to go back to his truck. Not to leave. He's no coward. Instead, to get a tire iron from his delivery truck. It would suffice on short notice for a weapon.

■■■

Carlos Mehia is trepidatious about the paramedic being able to administer the sedative to Decomp John. The paramedic is slight of build and Decomp John is clawing at the window to get out.

My name's Dino, he offers. What is this guy on? Dino asks.

Nothing. He's been bitten by a sick woman, Carlos volunteers, knowing it must sound crazy.

At that Dino's dark eyes sparkle with, You mean, like a zombie bite? Dino is from New Jersey originally where life is a lot harder he feels. He takes what people say in the South with a grain of salt. He keeps to himself that he thinks what Carlos is saying is balderdash. Though he does say aloud, I'll take my chances. I'm not kinemortophobic. He doesn't think Carlos will know what that word means, but he's mistaken.

It's no phobia if the condition is reality, Carlos says grimly. Then he remembers the memento mori walking stick in his trunk. Hold on, let me get something first. For our protection. Even though he thinks Dino's kind of being a smart ass, he doesn't want him to be killed by Decomp John and it is impressive that Dino knows a word like kinemortophobic.

Yeah, well, doubt I'll need anything besides this sedative, Dino jeers. I'm used to dealing with people on heavy duty street drugs not some white collar guy who tried a party drug for the first time, Dino now shouts back to Carlos rudely, as Carlos is getting the walking stick out of his trunk.

Dino foolishly doesn't heed Carlos's warning or even wait for Carlos. Instead, he opens the car door to administer the dose to Decomp John by himself.

Decomp John lunges for Dino and manages to push him down on the asphalt. Dino's a small guy, so it wasn't really that difficult, and Decomp John's super motivated, as he's hungry for Dino's flesh. As good as the Italian Meatball Sub tasted to Dino hours earlier, Dino tastes to Decomp John.

Debissa pulls up to Grimball Hospital about the same time Dino is being eaten alive by Decomp John, but she is on the other side, the Administrative Section where her sister works. Debissa can't process fully what had happened with their cousin, Principal Kasey Drope. She's just happy to be waiting on her sister at the hospital where she thinks it's safe. And, she doesn't plan on returning to ECHS till it's safe. They don't pay her enough to risk her life, she feels. She hopes Tara isn't late. She wants to hear what Tara thinks about what transpired. Then she gasps, as she remembers Mel. Recovering quickly, however, she thinks well, he's on his own now…cousin or not, she's not going back to ECHS.

May I? Luis asks, as he gently reaches for Graciela's heel and then takes it from her hand. He doesn't want her to endanger herself by going after Decomp Lou with just a shoe! Yet, that's what he's bravely going to do. Lee and Gianna wouldn't have acted so rashly, but since Luis has (prompted by Graciela), they have his back. Though with what weapon they have no clue. They look around the principal's office and spot some trophies in a glass case. Gianna takes off her shoe and smashes the glass case. The loud noise of shattering glass causes Decomp

Lou to stop his feeding on Principal Drope and look at the four teens with lifeless eyes.

They don't smell good to him. Unappealing. Not at all yummy, his decomp brain thinks. Makes sense as Graciela is a vegan (which as an aside reminds Luis of his mother which makes him even more protective of her), Luis is a vegetarian, Lee is a vegetarian and Gianna is a vegetarian. And, vegans and vegetarians aren't appetizing to Decomps. Only meat-eaters are appetizing to Decomps.

However, Luis doesn't know that he and his friends aren't meal-material for Decomp Lou, so he's even more apprehensive when DL stops munching on Principal Drope to stare at them with dead eyes. Luis decides that if he dies saving Graciela and his friends, then so be it. So, he flies at Decomp Lou with Graciela's heel. It sinks into DL's temple, and he utters a nightmare-inducing mewling cry. It's creepier than if it had been a forceful cry. A decomp no longer has functioning nociceptors, so they don't feel pain. The mewling cry they sometimes emit with their final death is more like an infantile lamenting of their short-lived second life. With that awful sound, Decomp Lou dies the second and final death.

Seeing DL now slumped over in death, the four friends breathe a sigh of relief almost in unison. Lee and Gianna are still holding trophies they'd confiscated from the glass case. The four feel flooded with relief, giving no thought to Principal Drope who would have died one and only final death due to his massive heart attack if he hadn't been infected by Decomp Lou. DL facilitates Principal Drope's new life: as an undead Decomp.

▪▪

When Mel tells his friends about having to call 911 after his uncle, Principal Drope, became unconscious, they don't believe him. Pushing his leather cowboy hat back to better look up at Mel since Connor is even shorter than him, he taunts, Yew shar it warn't jest weeshful thinkin'?

Connor likes to think he speaks with a cool dialect, but many would disagree.

The term 'friends' is one that is used quite loosely with this group of Mel and his cohorts, as the more accurate term is 'narcissists in agreement,' at least most of the time---they clearly don't believe Mel this time, so they are falling out of agreement, as is quite common for those of their ilk. They have loyalty to themselves first and foremost. Always. They're only in agreement at times to benefit themselves. Not out of true friendship. In fact, the disagreement has become so strong that Connor and his cohort Dottie are becoming increasingly intent on proving Mel wrong. So, they decide to go to Principal Drope's office and see for themselves. Mel shuffles along with them so as to see their faces when he proves them wrong.

Mel, Connor and Dottie arrive at Principal Drope's office about the time that now Decomp Drope raises his head in his second life as one of the undead and peers with his one uneaten eye at the human gathering. Lee notices his ghastly resurrection first, alarmed obviously. He touches Gianna's arm lightly to appraise her of the situation. Then she touches Graciela's arm. Graciela gasps with, Ermagd, not again. Luis watch out!

Luis had been trying to find something in Drope's drawers to wipe off Graciela's heel. Unsuccessful, the gore is still dripping down her heel-turned-weapon when he backs away from Decomp Drope quickly.

Luis was so close to Decomp Drope that he could have easily been DD's next meal, but DD doesn't like the way Luis smells…or Graciela…or Gianna…or Lee…no, but those standing behind them at the entrance of the office smell delicious to Decomp Drope. Those three smell better in fact than bacon to a meat-eating human.

Shuffling past the non-meateaters, Decomp Drope lunges for Connor. Connor ducks, true to

his cowardly nature, and lets his fuck-mate
Dottie get mauled by Decomp Drope. Connor,
intent on saving his own ass, turns around and
runs out of the office... then he runs out of the
school building to make sure he's safe from the
zombie. But, in his haste to get to his pickup
truck, he trips over his own feet and onto the
unforgiving asphalt. Bracing his fall with his
hands, the black, gritty paving slides under his
skin, cutting both of his palms open and leaving
inky gravelly bits floating under his skin. The
blood quickly forms around the little raised
black islands in his hands. He's going to need
stitches. That's for sure. Good thing, he thinks,
that Grimball Hospital is so close by.

Meanwhile, Mel had the same idea that Connor
did. Instead of helping his supposed friend,
Dottie, Mel just rubs in his being correct to her
by saying, Wha-le ah gaysss it warn't no hart
attacke afeter all, as he scoots away from the
office. It's the fastest he's moved in a long time.
Running out to the parking lot, he doesn't see his

cousin Debissa's car anywhere. All he sees is a bleeding Connor.

Connor looks at Mel, blurting out, luhk, yew dohn't have a rad nowe ase Derbissah's car ain't hare an' Ah cooed use thir hayelp.

Mel jeers, Sew yew're sayin' thayte Ah'us raht theyn?

Yays…nowe layt's git goin'… Connor emphasizes, as he tosses Mel the keys to his truck. So, within minutes Mel is driving the bleeding Connor to Grimball Hospital. Connor pulls out a beef jerky bar to eat along the way, not offering to share it with Mel.

About that time, Thomas McPherson comes in the office with his tire iron. He had no idea that Debissa was talking about a zombie, but he's no coward, and he truly loves his son, so there's no way he's leaving the situation at hand, so to speak. He doesn't know who Dottie is, but her screams are curdling his blood. So, without

94

hesitation, he sinks the tire iron into Decomp Drope's rapidly decomposing head. DD has already scratched Dottie's arms and sunken his gnarly teeth into her neck. As DD is dying his second and final death, complete with the sickening mewling cry, Mr. McPherson tells Lee to get Dottie to the infirmary. Okay, no big deal, Lee retorts, BUT she's been bitten. You think that's wise?

Yeah, Luis chimes in. She could turn into that. He points to the now unanimated body of Decomp Drope.

Still, we don't know what we're dealing with, Mr. McPherson stresses. We can't just kill her because we think she'll turn. We'll go to the infirmary together. And, if she turns, then I have this, he offers, holding up the bloodied tire iron. And, we have these, Lee volunteers. He, Luis and Gianna have taken trophies from the shattered case to use as weapons---just in case. They look at Graciela who offers, Think I'll be fine with my heels. She slips back on the bloody one Luis hands her. Luis decides he'll use the trophy as a weapon, perhaps, in the future, though Graciela's heel had certainly worked for him, too.

Graciela jokes with a stressed smile, Desperate times call for unfashionably gross measures, as she looks down at the bloodied heel/instrument of death she's now wearing.

■■

Seeing the 'zombi' (Carlos thinks in Spanish when highly emotional, and he doesn't think offhand at this point of Juan/John being a certain kind of zombie: a decomp) attack Dino so viciously, he realizes he needs to call his friend, Thomas, and tell him NOT to bring their sons to the hospital after all. He is scared for their lives now. He doesn't realize that decomps (this particular kind of 'zombi') are only interested in eating meat-eaters. He hasn't been able to process all he's seen yet. It's all been happening at such a fast pace that he's only been able to react to one horrifying situation at a time. He reaches Thomas on his cell phone as they

(Thomas, Lee, Luis, Graciela, Gianna and sickly Dottie) are walking to the infirmary. Bueno, Tomas, soy yo Carlos. Thomas knows his friend well enough to know he speaks in Spanish or Spanglish to him only when he's either under duress or when extremely happy, and this isn't one of the happy times. I'm sorry, Carlos continues in English, it's not safe for nuestros hijos 'aquere' (cross between aqui and here). Don't come to the hospital! Let's meet back at my beach house.

Normally I'd say of course, Thomas responds, then motioning for the group of kids to walk ahead before lowering his voice with, but George and Marjorie are missing. Their aviary was damaged from the hurricane. I'm worried about our other birds. I need to check on them. And, he adds in a still lower voice, Please say nothing to Lee about George and Marjorie just yet. I haven't had time to break the news of their disappearance to him yet.

Claro que yes! Carlos responds in his Spanglish.

A hospital security guard had been called a few minutes into Decomp John munching on Dino. As he was technically on call for 24-hours but could also eat lunch and dinner when things are slow, Cody was finishing up his juicy burger smothered in bacon with his girlfriend, Tara, when he gets the call. Time had been moving slowly for him, so this is welcome news for the thrill-seeker he is. He excitedly shoots a glance at Tara across the table, who is still devouring her meat burger, saying with his expression, *Wanna go with?* She had her burger prepared the exact same way. In fact, they had bonded over their love of eating murdered pigs and the fact that they were both adrenaline junkies. Of course, she wants to go with! Excitement! The opposite of her boring administrative duties. She doesn't think she'll be in any real danger. She calls Debissa, her sister, to tell her to pick her up on the other side of the hospital today. She has no idea that Debissa was already at the hospital or what Debissa had experienced earlier at ECHS.

Seeing Cody and Tara arrive at the grisly scene of Decomp John munching with gusto on Dino, Carlos feels he can leave. Careful to put his memento mori walking stick on his passenger seat first, he gets in next and starts his car. He's going to definitely be driving with the windows down to air out the heinous zombi scent. He shouts to Cody and Tara as he leaves, Cuidado this es a zombi! Then he pointedly stares at Decomp John. In case they can't figure out the former human munching on a human situation themselves! He would have stayed to see if he could help more, but he doubted he could with the condition of his knee, and he had Thomas and the boys to think of.

At the infirmary, Thomas and the teens leave a suddenly sleepy Dottie with the school nurse. Keep her in restraints, Thomas urges the nurse. There's a strange sickness going around. Turns people into cannibals, I think. Please be careful!

The nurse looks at him like he's a madman, but she keeps her voice steady to say, I'll give her a sedative.

A sedative?! Gianna scoffs, backing up Lee's father. It better be for a large animal because you're dealing with a potential zombie! And, it's not the normal kind, if there's even such a thing as a 'normal zombie'; rather, it's a rapidly decomposing but still super powerful one. It's a Decomp!

The nurse rolls her eyes. She doesn't like Goths like Gianna and their obsession with death, in this particular case the Goth girl was clearly into death via zombies. Graciela pulls Gianna's arm in a let's-go-don't-waste-your-time-with-an-ignoramus manner. Then turning to the nurse, Graciela chimes in with, Don't say we didn't warn you! The nurse doesn't care for trans kids much either, and for the second time in the span of a minute, she rolls her eyes.

Seeing the eye roll for the second time, Graciela breaks out into the lyrics for a new song she'd been working on the other day---inspired by the cute cat ears' headband she'd been wearing:

Best to be a cat without being catty.

Best to be a bat without being batty.

Best to be a dragon without being too fiery.

Best to be a girl who doesn't take it too personally!

Gianna smiles at Graciela with amusement and respect. Graciela could clearly lighten any mood, even in a life or death situation. Truly a friend worth having!

Nurse Arnotte had just finished eating some venison jerky, her hunter husband had recently made, before the sick student was brought to the school infirmary. It was just to snack on, but she enjoyed it so much that she figured she'd have it for dinner, too.

She leaves Dottie on one of the recovery couches in a closed off room, as she goes to her desk to look up Dottie's mother's number on the computer to come and get her as is the protocol. Dottie falls fast asleep about the time Nurse Arnotte reaches an annoyed Ms. Swilla Redcuella (she was never married to Dottie's father: Carl Asseley). Swilla only lives about five minutes from ECHS, but she was in the midst of giving her new boyfriend, an old paunchy handyman named Jimmy Arsender, a blow job. So, she is annoyed at the coitus interruptus (of sorts).

Swilla stomps into the high school to get her daughter. She's just about at the infirmary when she hears a blood-curdling scream. Not afraid, though she should be, she charges into Nurse Arnotte's office area. Blood is splattered on the wall, her desk and her computer. Nurse Arnotte's blood. Flowing freely compliments of

Swilla's newly turned daughter: Decomp Dottie. Waat arrr yew dewin', Dahtie? Swilla drawls. Decomp Dottie stops spewing viscera from her maw long enough to look up at her mother. Decomp Dottie tries to communicate with her mother. She manages to get out, Aaaaaaaaaaarrrrghhhhh. Nobody speaks fluent Decomp, but it seems her 'zombie speak' may have a bit of a drawl to it. And, as this is no 'zom com' or 'zomedy,' Dear Reader, I'll leave further commentary on this situation right there.

Help me, Nurse Arnotte pleads, though her mauled body is beyond any repair. I should have listened to those kids, she says with regret.

What kids? Swilla asks.

The Goth girl…Gianna…and the Trans boy…I mean girl…Graciela and the boys they hang out with. These are the last words Nurse Arnotte utters before she passes out from the pain of being eaten alive. Instead of stopping her daughter from finishing her gnarly human feast or calling out in the school for help, Swilla focuses on what Nurse Arnotte said about Gianna and Graciela. She doesn't like them either. She erroneously feels they're behind all this. And, she knows where one of the 'boys they hang out with' lives. The one who lives in the yurt. One of Jimmy's handyman jobs was dropping off the yurt. Jimmy'd told her all about the weird birds they keep there, too. 'Strange birds' those humans are! Many of those in Swilla's church have commented. Swilla remembers thinking, *Whew kapes berds ase payets?! Berds arrr jist fer ating. Hir gud lawerd Jeesus put aneimalls on irth jist fir hoomans ter ate.* She intends to go pay what she considers 'the troublemakers' a visit. She calls her boyfriend, Jimmy, with a cloying voice. "Jeemie sweetie, Ah neede yew hare now." He agrees to meet her at the school infirmary, Then, not knowing exactly what to do with her flesh-eating decomp daughter, she just shuts the door to the infirmary. That suits Decomp Dottie just fine as she's still rapaciously gobbling down Nurse

Arnotte. She'll deal with her zombie daughter later.

■■■

Jimmy is singing an oldies tune when he enters ECHS. He fancies himself a ladies' man even to teenage girls, so he took time to preen his whitish-grey beard (that was as thick as Santa Claus's) and brush his seriously discolored teeth before he left. He always keeps his beard to hide his raging case of rosacea. Nothing he can do about his rosacea flare-ups besides not drinking. But, that isn't happening, as Jimmy is a certifiable alcoholic who takes to Twitter to rant about one thing or another when he's two sheets to the wind. Which is quite in keeping with his also being a blowhard, as he boastfully assures everyone he meets that he's a good person. Jimmy thinks it's strange that he sees blood on one of the interior walls after entering the door to the high school, but he shrugs it off and heads to the infirmary to see Swilla. What he can't shrug off as easily is the student with dead eyes clawing at him right before he gets to Swilla, who is now standing right outside of the infirmary. Jimmy wishes he had his flask with him to take a swig, but instead, he just jabs the weird kid in the gut (the sickly kid falls and Jimmy just leaves him there). Then Jimmy rolls down his sleeves and greets Swilla.

Thank yew, Jeesus, Swilla exclaims, giving Jimmy a hug, thinking nothing of the fact that he'd just been scratched, or that the weird kid that Jimmy had just jabbed in the gut was getting up or that her daughter had turned into a zombie. No, she has only the meddlesome foursome (Gianna, Graciela, Lee and Luis) on her monomaniacal mind. Layts git outta hare, Jeemie. We got ter git tew thee wiredo MacFeersuns ASAP. I got a bone ter peeck weeth thim.

They hurry out to the high school parking lot. Swilla decides to drive, so Jimmy leaves his vehicle at ECHS. Suffering with major misplaced anger, all Swilla can think about is:

Jest wayte teal Ah givumm a peece a mah myend.

CHAPTER 9: (FROM NARRATOR'S POV AND CARLOS'S POV) "Bird Brains"

Some time before Dottie and Nurse Arnotte had turned to decomps, Thomas McPherson had left ECHS. Lee, Luis, Gianna and Graciela had also departed. Here's exactly how it happened: Mr. McPherson had originally planned on just taking Lee and Luis back to the yurt, but the recent cannibalistic events changed that. He had looked at the girls and said, I'd feel better if you came with us, too. At least till we know what we're dealing with. The girls agreed, deciding they'd each take their own vehicle there. Transportation options are always a good thing, especially in a potential zombie apocalypse, they all agreed. Since Gianna and Graciela didn't know exactly where Lee and his father lived, it was decided that Lee would ride with Gianna and Luis would ride with Graciela. Mr. McPherson had put his bloodied tire iron on the passenger side floor of his truck and took off first. He wanted to get to their yurt first to check on the situation with their bird family. Lee and Gianna rode in Gianna's vehicle with their trophies-as-weapons with them. Luis and Graciela rode in Graciela's vehicle with his trophy and her heels as weapons, just in case.

Thomas is checking on Setra, Jetavi, Philyra and Demisi when Gianna and Lee pull up to the yurt. He's taken the tire iron with him just to be on the safe side. About 10 minutes later, Graciela and Luis arrive (Graciela is a slow and careful driver). My father must be checking on our birds, Lee surmises, and he decides to wait at the yurt with Gianna till Graciela and Luis arrive.

Gianna thinks it's so cool and incredibly not-mundane that the McPhersons have birds, including turkey vultures, as pets. She also knows that the saying 'bird brain' as an insult is ridiculous, as many have remarkable avian skills. However, she smiles a bit considering that 'human bird brains' are an entirely different matter. They are oftentimes much more inept than feathered friends.

This way, Lee gestures, when Graciela and Luis arrive. He leads his friends down a rough-hewn path toward the aviaries. About the time Lee, Luis, Gianna and Graciela get to the aviaries to see a worried Thomas McPherson (as George and Marjorie have still not returned), a fuming Swilla is pulling up to the yurt with a sleeping Jimmy in the passenger seat of her car. She's angry at the what-she-considers-no-good teens (Lee, Luis, Gianna and Graciela). To add to that, she's pissed off that Jimmy has fallen asleep on the drive from ECHS to the McPherson's place. Swilla pokes Jimmy in his ribs, but he is sleeping soundly, even drooling a bit. Something that he does regularly. Shaking her head, she rolls down a window for him for air, and she decides to confront the what she considers meddlesome teens by herself. She knocks on the door of the yurt, but nobody answers. Then she hears noise coming from the aviaries so she heads off in that direction.

When Carlos left Grimball Hospital, he decided to stop by a store to stock up on supplies before heading to the McPherson's place. If there is a zombie pandemic about to break out, then fresh water and food (especially for vegetarians and vegans with an obviously more limited diet) will be more difficult to come by. He didn't even want to think about the infrastructure being in danger as a whole: cell towers, roads, et cetera. *Una cosa at a time,* he thought in Spanglish.

George and Marjorie, Lee starts…

I'm sorry, his father grimaces. Hurricane Willa damaged their aviary. They're not here. I'm hoping they're still alright and just left home due to being frightened. They're homing pigeons, so they should come home…

They're family, Lee states crestfallen. At that, Gianna steps beside him and takes his hand with a squeeze of heartfelt support. The others?

Fine, his father says quickly. Take a look for yourself.

At that, Philyra, Demisi, Setra and Jetavi all look at Lee intensely with their heads cocked to the side as if to say, We know you're talking about us, and don't worry…we're fine.

▪▪▪

When Carlos finally gets to the yurt with all the supplies, he tries knocking on the door, but nobody answers. He looks around the yard and sees Thomas' truck and three cars. He wonders who they belong to, but as nobody is in them, he just shrugs and decides to head to the aviaries, as he hears voices coming from that direction. Sounds like somebody is shouting!

▪▪▪

Carlos was right. Swilla couldn't control her misplaced anger any longer when she saw Lee, Luis, Gianna, Graciela, Mr. McPherson and the remaining birds at the aviaries. Yew…yew madeling keyads (her backwoods' accent had

113

gotten even stronger since she was extremely amped), she'd yelled, whaat exactly deed you dew ahat theh skewl terday?

Graciela looks at Luis with appreciation and pipes up with, Uhm…do you mean like him saving us from a decomp thingy? 'Cause to me that's heroic! Luis beams at Graciela. Graciela then breaks out into an impromptu song:

Whether he is battling bullies or zombies

He's the best, as cowardice is not in his wheelhouse~~~

Swilla glares at Graciela, as Luis, Gianna and Lee look on admiringly. Even Thomas McPherson smiles. Graciela has a lovely voice. She's the frontwoman (frontgirl) of a band called 'Clearly Grey' when not in the midst of what's looking a lot like the beginning of a zombie apocalypse.

Swilla is about to give them more of her uneducated mind when her former boyfriend, now Decomp Jimmy, comes ambling from the rough path (from the yurt to the aviaries) and lunges for her. Turns out, she shouldn't have left the window open for him. Jeemmmeeee, whate arr yew dewin?

At that, Decomp Jimmy makes contact with Swilla's mouth and starts munching on it. He forcefully pushes her to the ground, and within seconds, Swilla has no lips left to talk intelligibly. Of course, it could be argued that she had not been talking coherently for pretty much her entire life. He goes for her small brain next.

It's then that Carlos arrives at the aviaries and quickly tries to get Decomp Jimmy off of Swilla, as he's closer to them than the teens and Thomas are, having just emerged from the path. Even with his challenging knee situation, he manages to disengage Decomp Jimmy's teeth from the bloody hole housing what's left of Swilla's brain matter. Decomp Jimmy jerks around still chomping on her brain, and part of her brain dislodges from his mouth and accidentally flies with force to land on the ground in front of where the four teens are standing. It that respect, Swilla certainly did give them a piece of her mind.

Unfortunately, with his mouth now freed from chewing, Decomp Jimmy accidentally bites Carlos's hand. Decomp Jimmy would not have bitten Carlos on purpose, as DJ only thinks meat-eaters are appealing to eat.

Luis sees his dad's bleeding hand and starts to go towards him. Carlos shouts to him, Don't mijo!

Dad, don't be…don't be…searching for a word that will both keep his dad with him and impress him, he can only think of farfelu. Dad, please don't be…don't be farfelu!

Carlos smiles proudly at his son's word choice even under duress, yet his mind is already made up. He must leave to protect his son and his friends. With a mirthless smile, he thinks, *Pues, that went down hill quickly.*

Luis only concedes to his dad's wishes because Graciela is pulling on his arm to hold him back. Carlos smiles at Graciela. He sees what his son sees in her. He's known about the two of them for some time, but he's been waiting for Luis to bring up the subject. Carlos already knows what he'll tell Luis when he shares that she's trans. Carlos already has his probably lame-to-his-son joke ready. He's going to say something like, Of course I approve of her, as I'm trans, too: a trans-humanist. At that, Luis will roll his eyes, but be happy that his dad is so accepting. Now Carlos doesn't know if this conversation will ever come to be, but at least he knows Luis is in good hands with Graciela, Thomas and Lee.

Before Luis changes his mind and darts after him, Carlos moves as fast as he can with his knee issue on the rough path back to his car while shouting behind, Tomas, take care of mijo! Luis's friends encircle him with love and to keep him from changing his mind.

At the same time Luis's peers are encircling him, Thomas moves towards Decomp Jimmy with the tire iron and sinks it deftly into his head. He decides to put Swilla, who's now fallen unconscious, into George and Marjorie's empty aviary. Thomas can't help thinking with an inward smile that Swilla and Decomp Jimmy are 'human bird brains.' His real feathered family are much kinder and wiser than these good-for-nothing human-zombies (Swilla hadn't turned yet, but she was already a zombie in many ways). True 'bird brains' are much smarter than most realize. Philyra and Demisi are watching Swilla carefully. As turkey vultures, they feel that Swilla may make for a tasty meal at some point. But that, Dear Reader, is subject matter for another book. By contrast, Setra and Jetavi are wary of the sleeping Swilla. As rock pigeons, they don't find her appetizing in the least. Philyra and Demisi look at their feathered friends, Setra and Jetavi, as if to say: *No worries, feathered family...we'll protect you!*

Thomas gets Lee, Luis, Gianna and Graciela to help him repair the aviary. They are all hoping they can reinforce it before she awakes, as it's quite likely she's turning into a decomp as well. Not the greatest plan, but short of killing a woman who was still technically human, it's the only thing he and the teens could think of on super short notice. *Maybe there's a way to reverse the sickness?* Thomas questions internally, as they're making the repairs. He doesn't dialogue internally as much as his son, but he tends to question internally quite frequently.

∎∎∎

Cody is having a hard time trying to pull Decomp John off of his meal: Dino. He looks back at Tara pleadingly and then says demandingly, A little help here!

Tara claps back with, Yeah, well, I'm not exactly sure how to help. But, she tries to pull Dino out from under Decomp John with her right arm. Decomp John stops mid-intestinal munch to sniff the air. Something smells even better than his Dino-meal: Tara! Since Tara and Dino are both meat-eaters, it's perhaps strange that Tara smells better to Decomp John. However, the answer this admittedly self-proclaimed omniscient narrator has arrived at is: Because Tara recently ate a meat-meal, she smells like fresher, and therefore more appealing, human meat to Decomp John.

Debissa had driven to the other side of the hospital, per her sister's request, and she has arrived just in time to see Decomp John take a bite out of Tara's arm. The same one she'd used just seconds before to wrench a now-dead Dino out from under him.

Debissa opens her car door and screams to her sister, "Whate arr yew doin', Tarah? Git awaye frem thate thang!" Debissa is shocked to see what looks like another zombie here at Grimball Hospital, too. So, it's not a localized outbreak. It's not just at ECHS. As Tara is one of the few people Debissa really cares about, she motions for her sister to get in her car. A bleeding Tara begrudgingly gets into the car with her sister, leaving her boyfriend Cody to fend for himself.

As Debissa is leaving the hospital with her freshly bitten sister, she's surprised to see her cousin, Mel, driving Connor's vehicle, pull up to the ER entrance. Feeling only the slightest pang of guilt, as she was supposed to give Mel a ride home from ECHS, she just waves to Mel frantically in a get-away-from-there motion, as he's pulled up right beside where Cody, Decomp John and now freshly turned Decomp Dino are.

Cody motions for Mel (he knows him since he's Tara's cousin) and Connor to come help him since his girlfriend has hauled ass with her sister. Mel and Connor are afraid to get out because of what they experienced at ECHS, but Connor's wound needs attending to, so they reluctantly park and get out. A little help, guys? Cody pleas, pushing both of the decomps back with each of his arms as they're both lunging for him now.

Cowardly Connor only offers, Surry, Ah neede ter git these tahken keer ev, as he starts scurrying towards the hospital door.

Cowardly Mel hesitates for a moment, since Cody is dating his cousin, but then just says, Ah'm weethe heyum. And, he starts shuffling, his normal gait, toward the sensor-activated sliding glass hospital doors.

Unable to withstand both Decomp John and Decomp Dino's relentless attacks, Cody falls to the ground and gets bitten on both sides of his neck within seconds.

Connor is signing in at the ER desk while Mel waits with him in clinical-looking grey room. He picks up a "Field and River" hunting magazine to look at the pictures of the dead animals killed while hunting. In a hospital, where lives are supposed to be saved, it's a travesty that a magazine like that is subscribed to by the ER Administrators. Mel's not much for reading. He's so engrossed in looking wistfully at the picture of the beautiful dead buck, wishing he'd been the one to kill it, that he isn't paying attention to whom is entering through the sliding glass doors. Thinking they're safe is a big mistake, as within minutes, Decomp John, Decomp Dino and newly-turned Decomp Cody have activated the motion-sensitive sliding-glass doors and have come ambling into the ER waiting area. There Decomp John, followed by Decomp Dino and finally Decomp Cody crash into Mel with a purpose from the front. Mel's own disgusting blood splatters across the picture of the poor dead buck as Decomp John's teeth make contact with Mel's thick forehead first, then Decomp Dino's teeth find his left shoulder and Decomp Cody's teeth find his right shoulder. Mel shrieks in terror, and Connor shrieks as well, not for Mel's sake but because Mel still has the keys to his pickup truck. He's going to need them to avoid what's looking more and more like a zombie apocalypse. So, he stands in front of the decomps chomping on Mel and selfishly demands, Heyy, taws me the kays to mah truhck.

Seeing that Mel can't, Connor tries to reach into his right pocket where he'd seen Mel place them. After all, the zombies are busy with Mel's upper half: his forehead and both of his shoulders. Unfortunately for Connor, Decomp Cody thinks he smells even better than Mel. Probably because he'd eaten meat more recently than Mel, as he'd had the beef jerky on the ride from ECHS to Grimball Hospital and both of his palms were still bleeding from the parking lot fall.

Lucky for Mel, Decomp Cody lunging for Connor, enables him to shake both Decomp John and Decomp Dino off of him. Unlucky for Connor, Decomp Cody has now knocked Connor to the floor and has managed to take a bite out of his left arm-the same one which had been reaching for the keys to his truck in Mel's pocket.

A profusely bleeding Mel knocks Decomp Cody off of Connor and he says, Waye gotter git outtah hare...theye ain't gonner see us lak theyus...they'ul keel uss. Agreeing, Connor

124

now bleeding in multiple places as well, from his parking lot fall and Decomp Cody's bite, starts heading out of the hospital with Mel-to his pickup truck.

Whare een theah werld are weah gonner goah? Connor questions.

Putting the keys in the ignition of the truck with his meaty hand after getting in and closing the door while Connor slams his shut, Mel cries out, as the places where the decomps bit him are getting increasingly painful, Ah, ah…have ane ayunt whew werks ate 'The Awfulle Wafful.' Shay maye bay able ter hayulp uss.

~~~~~~

Carlos hopes he can make it to his house before he falls unconscious behind the wheel---thanks to the accidental decomp bite from Decomp Jimmy. Carlos is alarmed to see ambulances everywhere on the roads. He gets stuck behind one about three minutes from his house. He gasps aloud when he sees an undead face with blood on its hands and around its maw claw at one of the windows in the back door of the ambulance. He has a feeling that things went super south at Grimball Hospital after he left.

Carlos is contemplating how he'll end his life…before he turns into one of those decomp horrors. Maybe one of his memento mori blades will do the trick, he muses grimly. It would certainly be fitting.

Soon he was carefully stepping over the even further decomposed delivery driver, Jo, he killed earlier in his house. It seemed like lifetimes ago, though it was, in fact, the same day. Carlos walked in a desultory fashion to his bedroom. That was unusual. He felt his brain functions actually slowing down. He felt like he must be talking in slow motion when he said aloud, *I feel so sluggish. Strange. The bite from the decomp must really be taking eeee-ffect nowww.* Plus, the flesh around his hand seemed to be crumbling away from the bite right before his eyes. *So…what's the word mijo says? Sooo…gnarl-*

yyy! Smiling at that word, Carlos decides he'll use the memento mori blade to kill himself after one final swim in the ocean, in a kind of 'Shedding Seppuku', he thought sluggishly, realizing that his analogy wasn't exact, but without the mental faculty to examine it further. Unlike those who threaten to commit suicide out of wanting to garner sympathy or control over others, yet never really plan on killing themselves, Carlos truly planned on following through with it. So, he changed into swim trunks as rapidly as he could considering his knee affliction and zombie-bite affliction. He was walking through the dunes to the ocean shortly thereafter. And, his slow-moving thoughts were considering a new plan. *What if he drowned in the ocean before he actually turned? What if he drowned while still technically a human? One less blade to clean for whomever found him that way*, he smiled, as he considered it. He has a wicked sense of humor upon occasion---that is, ever since Julia died. Her death had definitely changed him, and he looked forward to seeing her again…he believed he would…though he hated the thought of leaving Luis.

∎∎∎

I close my eyes floating on my back as the waves gently carry me up and down. I smile thinking that I've always been a thalassophile~~~Luis would be impressed with this word. But, wait, if I'm turning into a zombie, then how can I bring to mind a big word like thalassophile? I let the gentle waves rock me more as I ponder it~~~Hurricane Willa had come and gone some time ago now. It is peaceful here~~~and, instead of sweating profusely like pre-decomps had done, I am actually cool to the touch, but not cold, and feeling less hazy thoughts-wise by the moment. Something about being in this salt water is actually reviving me. I'm certainly not tired, so I have no desire to nap. I look down at my hand which had been bitten by Decomp Jimmy, and amazingly, it's starting to heal before my eyes…I still don't want to risk going around mijo, Lee, Thomas, Gianna or Gabriela, but it occurs to me that maybe I'm turning into a different kind of zombie. One that can heal in salt water and regain one's mental faculties? Espero que si! Looking down at my hand, which had been crumbling and shedding away mere minutes before, but is now completely healed, I surmise, *Yes, that's it...I'm a Crumbler...or a Shedder! Maybe, just maybe, this crumbler kind I am doesn't have the same fate as the decomps...though I am ravenous...not for human flesh...gross...no, es...es que yo deseo the kind of flesh like the one who bit me...tengo hambre de carne de decomps! Que jodienda!*

CHAPTER 10: (FROM NARRATOR'S POV AND LEXIE'S POV) "No Longer Latent Lexie"

Lexie looks around at the New York City (Manhattan) loft wistfully. It's been so long since I've been here, Lexie tells the real estate agent. The loft has high ceilings and is bright---thanks to the numerous windows. Lexie remembers the photo shoot with Thomas like it was yesterday. She bends down to rest on the large open window's frame and breathe in the city air. She's well over 6 feet tall, so she's happy that the window is higher up than many would like. She usually towers over most window openings. This one is perfect for her. It's been years since she kicked her heroin problem, but making the decision to leave her husband and their boy still haunts her. She knows it was for the best mentally but not necessarily emotionally. For any of them. When she kicked the heinous habit, she'd discovered that she liked trading. A lot. Cryptocurrency (mostly Alt Currency) became her passion. She invested in some, and perhaps most importantly, she learned how to make money selling right before bearish markets took hold as a trader. In fact, she'd made so much from the cryptocurrency markets that she can now afford to buy this pricey loft. And, even more lofts, if she wants. Her financial gain reverie is interrupted by the sound of flapping wings. Much to her surprise, and the shock of the real estate agent, two homing pigeons land on the sill beside Lexie's arms. Great gods, Lexie exclaims with a broad smile as she would recognize them anywhere, George and Marjorie, what are you doing here?

~~~~~~

Joey is happy to have dropped off his shipment. Now, pulled over at a dirty truck stop in Winston-Salem, North Carolina, he can finally eat his fish from Smythe's. It smells weird, but that doesn't stop him from digging into it. Sanitary isn't his strong-suit. He decides he'll take a quick nap after eating. Suddenly, he's damn tired and starting to sweat profusely. He rolls down the window to his truck and tilts his seat back for some major shut eye.

****

It didn't me long to figure out something must be wrong for George and Marjorie to have flown back all the way to New York. After all these years! Maybe it was from the upheaval from Hurricane Willa I'd heard about on the news? From what I understood a Category One Hurricane wouldn't do much damage, but who knows?! I am no expert in that arena. I am an expert in trading cryptocurrency at this point, but I am not even primarily a fundamental trader, so I couldn't say which alt currency will hold its value in the longrun. I know how to sell and buy according to studying prices on charts. Almost unbelievable that I just happened to be at that same loft, too, as I didn't even live there yet, but

I told the real estate agent I definitely wanted to buy it---thank you, cryptocurrency market and smart trades! I still sorta feel bad for all the retail traders who I was betting against---those who lost out on selling when I figured it was going to become a bearish market. However, they should have learned not to trade so emotionally and study how to trade by not risking too much from the start. While I was in recovery, I was determined to turn my life around, so I started really studying how to trade. I practiced on my MetaTrader Demo Account for months before I actually used any of my real money. I didn't have much money to invest, but I invested smartly and was in it for the long-run. So, that brings me to here. Marjorie and George are here with---looking at me fondly from the back seat of my new Jeep. I bought them a spacious cage before I left New York. I love being able to buy items supporting causes I love now. I love that Stella McCartney is a vegetarian design house, so I have no problem paying for items like the blouse from there I'm wearing. It cost over a thousand dollars, and I was happy to pay it. May not have been the best choice heading to South Carolina after a hurricane, but hey, it makes me happy.

I was worried about travelling with George and Marjorie at first, but I want to hand deliver them back to Lee and Thomas. They seem to be fine with the traveling. I love watching them drink the fresh water I get them by using their beaks like straws. They're still thirsty, so I'll need to stop for more water soon. They are such cool birds! And, I feel I'll be good travelling in the Jeep in case I have to go down any country roads on my way to try and find my son and Thomas. I was strangely redirected from my Maps App off course when I was about 9 hours into my drive from New York. There is some kind of outbreak being reported in parts of South Carolina primarily. Strange. *Maybe that's why Marjorie and George flew back to New York? Not because of the hurricane, after all?* It just makes me want to get to Edisto (the place I'd last heard Lee and Thomas are) all the more quickly. I look back at Marjorie and George again. They will need some more water first. Hopefully, the run-down truck stop I just pulled into will have some…

▪▪

I get out of my Jeep and stretch my long legs. I eye the restroom situation warily. I need to get Marjorie and George some water, but it looks a little run-down. I open the glove compartment in my Jeep and pull out my brass knuckles. Just in case. I tuck them into my jeans and lock the Jeep before leaving. I still have the soft doors on my Jeep, but I plan on changing them out for the hard doors before I get to South Carolina. I pass by some guy in his truck who looks like he's sleeping off a bad hangover. The kind with liquor sweats, as his thin, dark hair is damp and accents his pallor. Parked in front of him is some guy rocking out to his music so loud that his crucifix is swinging from the bass in his rearview mirror. The guy has his eyes closed and is getting into a mundane tune by Mashtt Boredum. I can't stand basic music, and the track's (and whole album for that matter) about as basic as they come. Trite track. Trite album (titled 'Going Nowhere'). And, probably a trite listener---guessing by the basic clothing the overweight middle-aged man is wearing: Basic shades. Basic hat (to cover his thinning hair?). Basic shirt. I could go on...I laugh at the music snob that I am, but 'life's too short to do basic shit' is about as good a motto for my life as any. By contrast, Marjorie, George and myself have been rocking out to the awesome music of Beltane and Gojira and all the way from New York!

■■■

In the ultimate act of malfeasance perhaps, when trucker Joey awakes as Decomp Joey, he crawls out of his truck window and searches for food: that is, meat-eating creatures still alive. Rapidly decomposing Joey breaks his collarbone after falling out of his truck and onto his right shoulder, but he doesn't care in the least. He starts shambling, with his right shoulder now slumped downward and forward, to the car of a man who smells delicious. Decomp Joey can't wait to sink his teeth into the middle-aged man, whose music is blaring as if in further invitation, and ravenously eat his flesh. Boydman Merda is still listening to Mashtt Boredum turned up loud, to the annoyance of all others in the parking area except Decomp Joey, with his eyes closed when Decomp Joey lunges at him through his open window, knocks off his mundane hat and takes his first bite of Boydman's head. Decomp Joey doesn't mind Boydman's now-thinned-further hair as he eats the fleshy part of his scalp and then his brains later on with relish. Before long, Decomp Joey is even eating Boydman's sausage-like entrails with gusto. That is, before he gets a whiff of something even more delightful-smelling to his decomp appetite. He gets up with part of Boydman's intestines hanging from his mouth and shuffles over to the Jeep housing George and Marjorie. Generally, George and Marjorie only eat the nutritious food of grains, seeds, greens, berries and fruit that Thomas and Lee give them.

However, when they fled Edisto after their aviary had been damaged by Hurricane Willa, they got hungry on their flight to New York, so they stopped briefly to eat whatever they could find. So, they found and ate earthworms and snails. That made them technically meat-eaters. At least for the time-being. The time-being that Decomp Joey got a whiff of their meat-eating selves in the parking lot of the truck stop. If the Jeep had the hard doors on, then maybe he wouldn't have been able to smell them, but their delicious meat-eating bird scent had wafted to where Decomp Joey had been eating Boydman Merda.

The truck stop bathroom is filthy, but Lexie rolls up the sleeves to her expensive Stella McCartney blouse to keep them from getting wet and fills her canteen with water from the one working faucet and heads through the parking lot to her Jeep. She knows something is terribly wrong when she sees the splayed open and partially devoured body, of the middle-aged mundane man, she'd seen earlier. There he is: obviously dead in his blood-splattered car. His mundane music is still blaring. With a twisted sense of humor, Lexie observes aloud, At least his situation is no longer mundane. He definitely got an exciting death. No humor next, however, when she sees some psycho pawing at her Jeep. She sets the canteen down and reaches in her pocket for her brass knuckles. What the hell? She shouts out to the psycho, unafraid.

••

Decomp Joey is having no luck getting to the birds even through the soft doors. Maybe if he'd had more time, then he'd have managed to, but he didn't. Hey you, Lexie blurts out. What the fuck are you doing to my Jeep? At that, Decomp Joey turns around. Boydman's entrails are still in his mouth. Lexie doesn't smell good to Decomp Joey as she's a vegetarian. Lexie is thinking she'd seen some weird shit when she'd been a heroin junkie, but never anything this weird!

Losing interest in Lexie, as she is not meal-material, Decomp Joey turns back around to keep pawing at her Jeep door. When Lexie realizes that he may be after Marjorie and George, she doesn't hesitate to spring into action. Literally! With a jump, her long legs take her to Decomp Joey's side. She pulls him around quickly and skillfully sinks her brass knuckles into the right side of his decaying temple, but not without him clawing her left arm in the process. She doesn't care about the gore, she cares about saving George and Marjorie!

Lexie doesn't stick around to call the police. She doubts they could help anyway. She doesn't want any other hindrances keeping her from reaching Lee and Thomas. She only takes time to wipe some of Decomp Joey's gore off of her hand and brass knuckles and to change out the soft doors for the hard doors on her Jeep. Before long, she's happily heading out of the gnarly truck stop. When she is almost out of Winston-

Salem she passes by a spiked head on a Baptist Church Steeple, and she shivers. Felt to her like whoever's head was spiked there was involved in shady, criminal dealings, like the kind she'd seen when a heroin addict. She sees a turkey buzzard pecking at one of the deceased head's extraocular muscles. It's the last one keeping the dead woman's eyeball in the socket: it's the lateral rectus muscle, to be exact, and it's slowly being consumed by the hungry bird.

~~~~~~

About to cross the border from North Carolina into South Carolina, Lexie is contemplating recent events with, *The truck stop incident was weird. That spiked head on a steeple was way weird. My scratched arm is weirdly throbbing. And, why do I have a feeling that things are about to get beyond weird?* Realizing that there's nothing she can do about it except to try and be there for her boy and Thomas, Lexie cranks up Beltane's "Medusa's Revenge" and puts the pedal to the metal of her Jeep.

CHAPTER 11: (FROM NARRATOR'S POV) "No Waffling at 'The Awful Waffle'"

When Lexie gets to the turnoff for Edisto on US-17 S at SC-174, she starts feeling super lightheaded and she notices that her hands are getting cold. She decides to turn into 'The Awful Waffle' there at the juncture to rest for a minute or two.

She checks on George and Marjorie who tilt their heads to the side as if in observation of her, as they coo to her in support as if to say, We're here for you as moral support 'cause it looks like you're going through something.

And, indeed she was. She was starting to have the same sort of symptoms Carlos had as he changed into a Crumbler/Shedder. Lexie is about to shut her eyes to try and nap to perhaps clear her foggy mind when an altercation at 'The Awful Waffle'-clearly visible through their large windows-is playing out before her formerly shuttered eyes. Wide awake now due to the scene unfolding, she watches with her mouth agape, and she starts to salivate.

~~~~~~

Mel and Connor had arrived at 'The Awful Waffle' about 10 minutes before a transforming Lexie pulled up. Bleeding all over the booth they sit at and sweating profusely, both Mel and Connor are in bad shape by the time the owner of 'The Awful Waffle,' Valerea, walks up to her profusely bleeding nephew, Mel, yelling, Whaht thee hayel ees gowin' ohn hare? Yew'r rownin' mah boothe wethe yer blud!

Mel pleads, Puleese Aint Valereah…Ah…, but then he's suddenly so tired that he has to lay his hemorrhaging decomp-bitten head on the table.

Connor's left arm is starting to throb where he was bitten, and he's trying to stop the profuse amount of blood flowing from his wound with the napkins from the stainless steel napkin dispenser on the table. He's drained the entire dispenser by the time Valerea has convinced her girlfriend, Kaylan, to wait on them.

Sew, whatcher gawna have terday? Besahdes awl ov hour napekeens? she guffaws. Lewks lak sum cawld wahtered dew yew gud, as she mobs up both sweat and blood from the table with her dishrag.

Connor manages to shake his head in a yes for the cold water, but no words come out, as he's suddenly so sleepy that he also has to lie his head down on the table. The cook, a cool country fellow named Marvin, eyes the situation with a frown from across the long laminate counter separating the front of the restaurant from his exposed stovetop grills farther back. Intuitively, he searches for his butcher knife. He's a meat-eater, but when he's off work, he only eats meat that he's killed himself, and he gives thanks to the animals respectfully who gave their life for his. Though, lately, he's been considering going vegetarian, as there are plenty of foods he realizes he can eat which are vegetarian with plenty of protein and taste, as much of the way meat-dishes taste are due to the seasonings and not the dead animal itself. Plus, Marvin likes his own four-legged animals (6 dogs and one cat), as they're more trustworthy and loving, far more than he likes most two-legged animals: humans.

Kaylan goes to throw her bloodied dishrag in the pile to be washed. It's one that Valerea has set up near the back door of the restaurant. Passing by where her much older girlfriend is-to get to the dirty stack of rags-Valerea stops Kaylan by putting her hands possessively around her waist. Then, she steals a kiss from Kaylan before she returns to the table with their now sleeping customers, Connor and Mel. Valerea then adds, Thahnks, Sweetee. Hay's mah nayphew, sew I gotter haylp.

Yew mahne, Ah gotter haylp, Kaylan corrects with a frown, scurrying to get away from Valerea. Ever since Valerea had her diseased gum issues, her breath has been less than desirable, to put it mildly. Though Kaylan's was also not-so-great as she'd had grilled onions with steak, 'The Awful Waffle' house special, for lunch.

When Kaylan gets to the table with a fresh rag, Decomp Mel awakes. And, he's hungry for what's not listed on 'The Awful Waffle' menu: meat-eating Kaylan! Kaylan's eyes widen in disbelief as Mel takes a bite out of the arm Kaylan was holding the new rag in when she had gone to clean up the table more in front of him. Kaylan screams in horror as blood spurts from her arm. At that bloodcurdler, brave Marvin springs, literally, into action, as he bounds over the laminate counter with his fortunately found butcher knife. Within seconds, Marvin sinks the knife into Decomp Mel's head with a, Dye undayed fuckerr! DM then lets out a mewling sound before leaving his short-lived second life.

Seeing the commotion inside, Lexie decides to lock Marjorie and George safely inside her Jeep and enter 'The Awful Waffle.' Decomp Mel's appearance has been strangely attractive to her. She has no idea why...

Kaylan is sitting down at a vacant table having wrapped the same dishrag, the one she'd used to clean up more of Mel's blood and sweat, around her freshly bitten arm.

As a spacey Lexie is being seated by Valerea, Decomp Connor raises his undead head from the table. Sniffing the air, he realizes he has a great human smorgasbord to choose from at 'The Awful Waffle.'

Seeing the newly-turned zombie sniff the air (Marvin doesn't think of them as Decomps, though they are), Marvin realizes he has to put his butcher knife to use again. So, shortly after Decomp Connor stands, trying to figure out who would make the best human meat-meal, Marvin sinks the knife deep into the middle of his head, destroying his deceased brain. DC lets out a pitiful mew and then keels over at the in-need-of-some-serious-cleaning table.

Shaking off the fog from her thoughts, Lexie starts worrying again about her son and Thomas. She needs to find them! Maybe someone at the police station would know where they are, or a school or maybe the hospital? She looks at the bleeding Kaylan, and asks, Do you know where I could find the police station or maybe the hospital…I'm looking for my son!

Kaylan looks at Valerea and demands, Ah neede tew git these lewked aht. Then, turning to Lexie, she says, Ah cude tahke yew tew thay hahspeetal eef yew geeve may a rahd. Kaylan doesn't have a car, and she gets a ride from Valerea everywhere generally. Valerea likes to keep her dependent that way. Still, Valerea doesn't need any more blood at her restaurant than there is already, so she agrees.

Kaylan falls asleep on the way to Grimball Hospital with Lexie, George and Marjorie looking at her curiously for different reasons. Prior to sleeping, Kaylan was sweating so profusely that even the air conditioner wasn't helping. George and Marjorie start eyeing the now sleeping Kaylan warily, while Lexie finds herself strangely salivating again and licking her lips.

Not knowing exactly where Grimball Hospital is since Kaylan fell asleep, Lexie pulls over. She still feels so spacey. She sees Kaylan start to stir, and she hopes that she'll be able to finish getting them to the hospital. Instead, Decomp Kaylan starts pawing at the cage housing Marjorie and George. Lexie is both protective of George and Marjorie AND suddenly so hungry that she bites into the left cheek of Decomp Kaylan. Lexie thinks it's a strange way to protect George and Marjorie, by biting and eating Decomp Kaylan's cheek, but she convinces herself that she must continue for their sake and because this Decomp meat tastes so delicious. Stronger than her human-self had ever been, Shedder Lexie, for that's what she's become thanks to Decomp Joey clawing her arm, pulls Decomp Kaylan's arm completely out of its socket to better have at it and starts chewing on and swallowing it next. Shedders are stronger than Decomps and perhaps even more ravenous.

As the gnarly, but delicious to Shedder Lexie, dead skin and tainted, but vital to SL, blood from

Decomp Kaylan slides down her throat, SL muses as her wits return full-force thanks to the feeding, *Yeah, I'd say all is way beyond weird at this point. So weird that even Rod Serling would've probably been shocked by this one.* And at that, much as a meat-eating human would eat a poor bird's wing, Shedder Lexie completely tears Decomp Kaylan's arm off and starts munching on what's left of it to tide her over till she can find Lee and Thomas. Resolutely, head clear now from her decomp meal, SL starts driving again.

When Decomp Kaylan starts loudly complaining at being 'eaten undead' by Shedder Lexie with, Arrgggh, arghhh, Shedder Lexie loses patience with her as she is trying to concentrate on the road. So, SL keeps her left hand on the wheel while she pulls out her brass knuckles with the right. Then, SL sinks them deeply into DK's rapidly decomposing brain. Seconds later, with a sickening mewl, Decomp Kaylan dies her second and final death, and Shedder Lexie licks all the undead blood and gore off of her brass knuckles like they're the best lollipop ever!

Glossary

(in Alphabetical Order)

***Spoilers galore here, so don't read this part until the end (unless you're into spoilers…hey, who am I to judge?!) or before your second reading, as it's to be used for clarification purposes primarily.

<u>Crumbler(s)/Shedder(s)</u>: Some will refer to them as crumblers, and some refer to them as shedders in my forthcoming novel(la) titled "The Aftermath" (working title). These are those former vegans/vegetarians who've become infected by a decomp bite accidentally. The decomps don't go for human vegans and/or vegetarians generally as they don't smell like food to them; the crumblers also don't go after either vegans or vegetarians. Seriously grotesque, however, is the fact that crumblers crave decomps. To eat! Crumblers are much slower to decompose than decomps. Yet, even crumblers will deteriorate within three weeks if

154

they don't bathe in salt water. However, they can theoretically live forever if they have decomps to dine on and salt water to bathe in. They are physically and mentally more powerful than the Decomps.

Decomps: These are the meat-eating zombies who were carnivores or omnivores while still human. They've been infected by a bite (or scratches) from another zombie or the specially-tainted seafood served at Smythe's. As their name suggests, they rapidly decompose. From the time of their turning (after their first death they are able to reanimate thanks to the meteoroid, but thanks to the cannibalistic lancet fish who ingested the meteoroid, they also have a craving for meat-eating humans) to their second (and final) death (as in no longer able to animate via any movement) is from 24 hours to three days max (unless killed by a human or crumbler first). This is due to the fact that they decompose so quickly. Also, there was no virus responsible for their creation; rather, they came into existence when the biological balance was disturbed when a tektite-like glass meteorite (which is alien to Earth) crashed into the Atlantic Ocean and a series of events spanning millions of years unfolded. Decomps only want to devour (from head to foot, not just the brain) meat-eating humans. They don't desire to eat vegans and/or vegetarians, as these humans don't smell right to them. Decomps also don't want to eat shedders (crumblers) or fellow decomps. A decomp no longer has functioning nociceptors, so they don't feel pain. The mewling cry they sometimes emit with their final death is more like a lamenting of their short-lived second life.

ECHS: Acronym for Edisto Cusabo High School

Grimball Hospital: a five minute drive from ECHS.

Hurricane Willa: This Hurricane is somewhat personified as a disruptive force/entity. Hurricane Willa hits the coastline of parts of South Carolina (Edisto Beach gets hit the hardest). Hurricane Willa is part of the reason that decomps and shedders (crumblers) arise.

<u>LS (Lucas Shipment)</u>: a parcel delivery company in the Southeastern part of the United States of America. Both Thomas McPherson and Jo Baumerde work there.

<u>Smythe's</u>: Renah's rundown restaurant on Edisto Beach that serves the tainted fish and chips.

<u>Tektite-like Glass Meteoroid</u>: it's a bright yellowish brown color (like a brighter topaz). It crashed into the Atlantic Ocean 15 million years ago unbeknownst to any human.

Character Profiles

***Spoilers galore here, so don't read this part at all before your first reading of this novella and if you don't want a few spoilers regarding the sequel to this novella.

Luis Mehia:

Physical Description: A 16-year old boy (when the Decomps and Shedders/Crumblers come into existence) with light brown curls and big dark blue eyes (the kind that change and many both girls and boys tend to swoon over) with thickly fringed brown lashes. He's already 6 ' 2" tall with a muscular build and could easily be a model.

Attitude: He's quick-witted, stands up for the underdogs, and likeable to everyone---except bullies and some zombies.

Best friend: Lee McPherson.

Occupation: Student (10th Grade), surfer, martial arts practitioner and destroyer of some zombies.

His favorite album is a retro one by the Butthole Surfers, *Electriclarryland,* mostly because of the track titled "Pepper" which in its being riddled with death makes him feel better about his own mom having died. He doesn't feel like he's alone in having someone near to him, his mother, dead when listening to it.

Luis is an extrovert who has no problem making new friends and keeping the old.

He deals with conflict well as far as eliminating as many zombies (see my sequel) as he can to protect his family. But, he is mourning the death of his mother internally---though he won't admit it (not to his father, Carlos Mehia, and certainly not to his classmates). So, he can be introverted when it comes to expressing his feelings about his mother's death---to his father and especially to classmates.

Though he wouldn't admit it to anyone, not even himself, his long term goal is finding a mother figure in his life. And, his short term goal is getting safe living quarters for his father, himself and friends after the zombies infiltrate their former beach house (again, spoiler of the sequel).

His best quality: he's loyal and doesn't desert those he loves. So, even though he really wants to get out of Edisto because it reminds him of his deceased mother, and plans on getting out when he graduates high school, he doesn't want to desert his father. So, he's conflicted.

His worst qualities: he's not always honest with himself in his desperate desire subconsciously to reconnect with a mother figure in his life. Plus, he overuses the word 'yeah' and tends to repeat himself to others and to himself.

Skills: He speaks both English and Spanish fluently, and he's skilled in martial arts. He's also a great surfer.

Nervous habit: he chews on the inside of his left cheek when anxious or pondering something.

He and his dad, Mr. Carlos Mehia, have a more relaxed relationship than Lee McPherson and his father.

He's a vegetarian.

Mr. Carlos Mehia: A great dad to Luis, wealthy (inherited a lot of money, but before that worked in a brick and mortar bookstore), animal rights activist, vegetarian/aspiring vegan. Still in love with his deceased wife: Julia. Julia died a little over three years ago (at the start of the novella).

Mr. Mehia is known for his largesse to animal shelters in the area and elsewhere---he gives to shelters in Julia's name (even though she's deceased).

Since Julia's death, he's become a collector of memento mori artwork.

He's fluent in Spanish and English, and he is a true gentleman with dark brown curly hair and large dark brown eyes.

When nervous, in either a bad way or good, he tends to speak in 'Spanglish.'

<u>Mrs. Julia Mehia</u>: She was a lawyer and animal rights activist. Beautiful on the inside and outside. She was tall, slim with blonde hair and big blue eyes. She is the deceased mother of Luis Mehia and was the wife of Carlos Mehia. She was adored by many and left a wonderful legacy of great work, et cetera. She was vegan.

<u>Lee McPherson</u>: Part of "The Upsurge" is from his point-of-view (in first person narrative). He's a 16-year old boy (in the 10th Grade at ECHS) who's had a rough life in some ways. He was once homeless (living under a bridge in Downtown Charleston for a stint with his father after their house was foreclosed on, et cetera). His model mother (in some ways) got hooked on heroin and deserted them, et cetera. He's remarkably tall (about 6' 8", so even taller than his best friend, Luis), lanky, a bit awkward, not always sure of himself, stoops out of not having the most self-esteem, but he has gorgeous big deep brown eyes that are almost hypnotic.

They're fringed with long dark lashes and a mop of thick dark hair. Think good- looking-poet type where the waters run deep. Like a young Antonio Banderas, but without the Spanish accent. He's a great surfer, too---one of the bonding points he and Luis have. He's searching for a mother figure, too, like Luis. Though his model mother deserted his father and himself and is still alive. Luis' mother only deserted through her death. Big difference there. But, both boys have ultra-supportive fathers in different ways.

His favorite album is, like Luis', a retro one: TSOL's (True Sounds of Liberty's) "Dance with Me." His favorite track from the album is 'Code Blue.'

Ironically, that's what happens to the dead (zombies) around him. They're fucked---though not at all in the same the way the dead are fucked in TSOL's track titled 'Code Blue.'

Language(s): He only speaks English and a bit of 'Spanglish' he's picked up from Luis and Mr. Mehia.

His signature look: Band t-shirts with jeans.

Skillset: He's great at building things and fixing things. Since he's been poor, he's learned how to make a lot of things to suffice.

Nervous Habit: He overuses the expression 'no big deal' (even when it is a big deal)---both to himself and to others.

He is more formal with his father than Luis is with his dad.

Fun fact: he amuses himself with his internal dialogue.

He's a vegetarian.

Thomas McPherson: Lee McPherson's dad. He works for LS company, but he used to be a male model when younger. He met Lee's mother, Lexie, on a photo shoot in New York City. They were working with homing pigeons on the shoot, as two model spies, and they both developed a great affinity for the pigeons. And, all birds for that matter.

Mannerisms: he sucks in his breath and puckers his lips when nervous and he mumbles to himself sometimes. Like when thinking of or reliving his dreams/nightmares in his mind. He's an Aquarius and he has prophetic dreams.

He generally has a nasal, Northeast United States accent, except when mimicking Southeasterners. He's not always PC. He feels like life's betrayed him in some ways. He comes across as gruff to many humans, but he's kind to furkids and featheredkids.

He's a vegetarian.

George and Marjorie McPherson: The McPherson's homing pigeons. They're family.

Jetavi and Setra McPherson: The McPherson's rock pigeons. They're family.

<u>Philyra and Demisi McPherson</u>: The McPherson's peace eagles (also known as turkey vultures). They're family.

<u>Lexie Dale McPherson</u>: Lee McPherson's mother. She is 6' 3" tall, so quite tall for a female, and a former model with beautiful long, dark curly hair.

Sun sign: Libra.

She got hooked on heroin, so she became an unfit mother. She felt it best for her son and husband to leave them rather than exposing them to the seedier side of life. She still loves both of them dearly.

She's kicked her heroin problem for good about three years before the zombie outbreak, but she didn't know if her son and husband would want her back in their life. When she happens to be at the same location George and Marjorie (the homing pigeons) return to after their aviary is damaged by Hurricane Willa, she bravely heads down South to see if she can hand deliver them back to her son and Thomas.

Signature Fragrance: Chanel's 'Chance.'

She's a vegetarian.

In the years since her recovery (from heroin), she's made a fortune in cryptocurrency (Alt Currency, specifically). She sold right before major bearish markets.

She's into non-mundane music---much like her son's love interest, Gianna. She likes less Gothic and more hard rock and metal, however.

Gianna Middleton: Goth girl, slender, tall, black hair (dyed that way, as it's really light brown), big light-blue eyes heavily lined in black almost all the time. She's highly intelligent, funny and fearless. She is Lee McPherson's love interest.

Strengths: Upstander, brave, into animal rights (she's a vegetarian).

Her favorite music: Anything that's NOT mundane. She loves Sopor Aeternus & the Ensemble of Shadows.

She's quite in touch with her 'inner child,' so she does not tolerate those who are disrespectful to her or those she loves for long.

She's fascinated with Bitcoin and other cryptocurrency.

Graciela/Grey: Transgender (MTF) character. Named Grey Ernesto Dulce on birth certificate. Graciela by choice. She's in the band rather eponymously named after her: Clearly Grey! She saves her friends/bandmates by using her heels to Decomps' heads (sequel spoiler). Luis's love interest. She's petite and partially Latina. She is about 5 feet without heels. She and Luis make a cute couple. Big height difference between them. She's in the 10th Grade at ECHS.

She's passionate about animal rights (she's Vegan) and gay rights (in that order). Her favorite song is Muse's "Uprising."

She's a bit prissy, but in a cute way. Likes current expressions.

<u>Mel Rene Paltry</u>: An 18-year old yokel-bully who has failed the tenth grade twice. He's slow-witted, and he represents the 'figurative zombie' sort before he becomes a 'literal zombie.' He's a malignant narcissist who only finds joy in trying to cut others down. He's a foil character to Lee and Luis.

He is prone to being apoplectic as malignant narcissists frequently are.

He's short.

<u>Connor Cravaho</u>: he's a high school bully (whose mother is rumored to be a Black Widow Killer with two husbands dying under suspicious circumstances in less than five years). He hooks up with Dottie Asseley regularly.

Even shorter than Mel.

<u>Dottie Asseley</u>: she's already a criminal at just 16-years old, as she's already blackmailing family members, et cetera. She's extremely overweight with dull brown hair.

Same height as Connor.

<u>Renah Lousquat Conoher</u>: She's the unappealing owner of Smythe's. She has dull-blue lifeless-looking eyes---even before the zombie apocalypse. She's been suicidal in the past and has blamed it on her exes every time, yet she's refused to get professional help when they've suggested it to her. Her lack of caring for herself has spread to Mother Earth, as she's a horrid litterbug.

Sun sign: Aquarius

<u>Mystilo</u>: weathered fisherman who's around 50 but he looks more like 70 due to fishing in the sun without sunblock. He's thin and wears baggy faded clothes. He's missing his front teeth due to them getting knocked out in a bar fight when he was younger. He regularly sells his unregulated fish for cash to Renah Conoher. She fries them up to serve to patrons at her restaurant, Smythe's.

<u>Evan Scourga</u>: fancies himself a pioneer in the occult arena. His father was a Mason who abandoned him, so he has an unfounded hatred

of Masons. He cyberbullies Masons regularly whilst only promoting his own thinly veiled agenda on social media. It doesn't take long for those around him to see his true colors, so he has a hard time keeping 'friends.' He has no true friends, just those in narcissist agreement with him. He's an egomaniac who's around 45 years old.

To say he has an 'Oedipus complex' is an understatement.

Sun sign: Aries.

He's an online cyberbully who enjoys puppeteering the clueless. Fancies himself a master of the esoteric, but his posts on Twitter are obviously exoteric-to those who're not puppeteered easily and can read right through them.

Lizzie Jado: she fancies herself a pioneer in the metaphysical arena. Yet, she's really a charlatan who reads people's cards (mostly in the astrological vein) for money. She doesn't really care about people, so she doesn't do it for free.

Also, she makes fun of those who give her money behind their back. Pretty on the outside with long auburn hair and a small frame (tends to use her 'thin privilege' to get what she wants: namely, chump clients), but ugly on the inside. She's around 40 years old, but she looks to be around 30.

She's also a litterbug.

<u>Joey</u>: a trucker who eats the tainted lancet fish. He's in his mid-30s.

<u>Jo Baumerde</u>: a butch delivery woman in her late 30s. Short and stocky. She's definitely not the sharpest tool in the shed. Meat-eater.

<u>Jennifer Chiste</u>: a femme woman in her early 40s. Needy. A former pastry chef who is now on social security. Her culinary concoctions were on the bland side. Tall. She weighs 300 pounds, but she's not the cool 'rad fattie' sort. Rather, she's clingy, complaining and unhealthy. Meat-eater.

<u>John</u>: aspiring vegetarian, but he's still a pescatarian. He is promoting the vegetarian meetups with Carlos Mehia.

<u>Principal Kasey Readylaw Drope</u>: corrupt, doughy, condescending, trite and pretentious principal at ECHS. He has a dismissive tone/attitude. He kills fawns and eats them regularly. He has heart disease. Unhealthy mentally and physically. Mel Rene Paltry is his nephew (his sister's son).

<u>Debissa Eastfoul</u>: frumpy secretary of Principal Kasey Readylaw Drope. She's also Principal Drope's second cousin. She's the first cousin once removed of Mel Paltry. She's a meat-eater and coward generally with the exception of saving her sister, Tara, who does not return the favor (hello, sequel).

<u>Tara LePew</u>: Debissa's sister. She works at Grimball Hospital. Meat-eater and coward. Throws her own sister under the bus, so to speak, to save herself from decomps shortly before she turns into one herself (hello, sequel),

as she was bitten by a decomp at Grimball Hospital.

Cody: Hospital security and Tara LePew's boyfriend. Meat-eater.

Nurse Arnotte: nurse at ECHS. She doesn't like Goths and/or Trans people. She's a meat-eater. Some of her favorite food: venison.

Ms. Swilla Redcuella: she is the mother of Dottie Asseley. She never married Dottie's father: Carl Asseley. Her current boyfriend is Jimmy Arsender. She's a meat-eater. She met Jimmy at a karaoke bar. Like her boyfriend, Jimmy, she fancies herself a great singer. She thinks that she can sing any kind of music---be it pop, soul, et cetera. However, everything that comes out of her mouth in song or speech is 'Pure T (not D) Country.' She's a bigtime bible thumper, and she's prone to mawkishness. Spoon fed lies online by cyberbullies with their own agenda. A puppet for the cyberbullies.

Jimmy 'HB' Arsender: Swilla Redcuella's boyfriend. He's a grizzled, paunchy handyman with a superior attitude who likes to say he's a troubadour, but he only sings covers. He's an alcoholic who suffers from rosacea. His 'friends' know he's been hitting the bottle when he has flare-ups with the rosacea and when he starts posting an exorbitant amount of misled and mundane observations he takes to be genius on Twitter. He's a meat-eater. He's also a braggadocious man who does it all under the guise of false humility. 'Humble Bragging' should be his middle name. He's been fed false information online which he willingly believed. He's a puppet for the cyberbullies' agenda.

Boydman Merda: loves listening to the mundane music of Mashtt Boredum turned up loud till Decomp Joey literally eats his mundane brain along with his other body parts. Middle-aged drab man.

Kaylan Patlame: Thumper femme woman, who tries to pass as decades younger by having dated much younger butch girls and using way too many filters on her Facebook page, yet she's now dating a much older femme woman named

Valerea for the both job and financial security. She works at 'The Awful Waffle' where Lexie stops.

Valerea Wadrelative: Kaylan Patlame's sugar mama. She owns 'The Awful Waffle' where Kaylan works. She's Mel's aunt.

Marvin Valiente: Backwoods and brave guy who works at 'The Awful Waffle.' Talks with a thick southern accent. Heroic in his actions. Deep thinker and willing to change his old ways for better ones.

"Malrenpar's Demise: A Smoke-Long Lagniappe"

***Trivia: I wrote this as a stand-alone fictional story, but it definitely fits thematically (and storyline-wise) with "The Upsurge."

Vladina felt the vampyre beacon sometime early Wednesday morning in her deep bedbox sleep in a lovely, recently renovated house she'd bought in Alexandria Bay. She'd often spent time there and in the Thousand Islands Area as a whole in the stifling heat of the summer and early fall. Her vampyre brethren, in the archaic sense of the word, were desperately calling out to her in the way that only vampyres and vampires could. Something about their food supply, humans, being in jeopardy from a new threat to vamp-kin. Many vampyres have prescience and therefore have foreknowledge of events in the near future. Vladina didn't hesitate to answer their beacon with her own to say that she was on the way, even though she truly hated having to return to the South…

That evening she flew as fast as she could, cloaked in the barely dusky sky, careful to avoid the just burgeoning moon's rays (as they reflected sunlight). She made it to Winston-Salem, North Carolina before her hunger became more than she could bear, and while it was still a deepening evening sky, as she knew she'd have to get a quick bite to eat due to the great energy she'd expended in such rapid flight, especially with her trusted and heavy sword, Juracia, in tow.

It was Wednesday evening, and a Baptist church service was just getting out. Plenty of pickings there, Vladina surmised. A short butch woman stood out to her with a heavily wrinkled face. The wo-man was also thin-lipped to match her thinning hair. She was about 50 years old (even though she was a butch, she was exceedingly vain, using multiple filters on both Instagram and Facebook to hide her sun-damaged and otherwise unremarkable visage and lumpy meatsuit which made her appear to be at least 65 in real life). Yet, she fancied herself quite the 'ladies' stud,' and she bragged she'd only go out with thin femmes, even though she didn't have much to offer, as she was poorly educated and collected social security since she was too lazy to work. Her name was Malrenpar, and she turned to criminal ways to make money on the side. She wooed women online who had successful careers and then tried to blackmail them with 'dirt' she tried to collect while dating them or just plain lied and made up about them when she couldn't find any. She'd use their telephone numbers and e-mail accounts to set up false pages on them. Criminal that Malrenpar was, she had no problem engaging in fraudulent activities. Plus, Malrenpar had recruited a group of like-minded criminals to aid her in trying to bring down her exes, but to no avail in most cases, as many savvy people could spot her criminal, malignant narcissist lies and false sites. Many bible thumpers were too ignorant, however, to do so, so they and the criminal human flying monkeys in her posse had a fairly significant presence in their uneducated circle.

This hypocritical circle, of Malrenpar and her criminal recruits, was congregated outside of the Baptist church, for their Wednesday night service had just gotten out. Vladina and her sword, Juracia, could easily feel the kinds of human shit they were, so it would have been easy to swoop down and just end their miserable lives right then and there and feel no remorse whatsoever in doing that, as that act would be helping so many lovely women who'd been victims of Malrenpar and her horrid posse's lies and criminal activities. However, just as Vladina was going to fly down to drain the fugly so-called 'stud' Malrenpar and her criminal group in front of the rest of the congregation freshly out of the chuch, Juracia started vibrating forcefully in her hand. And, Vladina took heed. Juracia wanted Vladina to let her kill Malrenpar, as she didn't want Vladina ingesting human crap like her. Then, Vladina had an idea…why not toy a bit with her first? So, instead of landing before the criminal group led by Malrenpar, Vladina landed just around the corner of the main door of the church, in a quiet area where she could compose herself a bit after her rapid flight from Alexandria Bay.

Vladina looked at her attire. Never mundane if she could help it, she looked like an Amazonian Goth Chick, so probably not the norm for a Baptist Church Service gathering in the South but not obviously vampyre either. Even though the bloodlust was already upon her, she controlled her eyes from red to black again and smoothed her long, black curls with her free hands, after she quickly placed Juracia in a scabbard behind her back which she'd recently picked up in a cool Pagan store in Alexandria Bay. Vladina was strikingly gorgeous, both in her symmetrical facial features and curvy strong frame. Yet, most who came into contact with her didn't dare admire her physical features overtly, as she was more glorious and deadly than the Goddess Kali. Vladina's mere presence generally demanded respect, unless one was too ignorant to realize it…

Hypocrites that they were, Marlrenpar and her flock of human flying monkeys and those who were fellow narcissists in agreement with her, had no problem discussing how they were going to try and extort money from Malrenpar's latest ex right in front of the Baptist Church. Malrenpar had already set up fake pages in her ex's name and was trying to win over her ex's family members with lies to try and give her lies more credibility. It wasn't working. Malrenpar didn't care in the least about the lives she was trying to ruin; she only thought about promoting herself via lies and trying to score more money illegally. Her paltry social security check didn't allow her the extravagant lifestyle that her malignant narcissist ego thought she was entitled to. Her criminal flock saw a potential way for themselves to make money, too, by joining in. Vladina and Juracia could feel the criminal energy of the low-life group grow stronger the closer they got to the criminals congregated just outside the church doors. In fact, shortly before discussing their latest plan of criminal attack, they'd been shaking hands with their senior minister. It's of note that the senior minister wasn't in Malrenpar's criminal posse, but the fact that his church attracted her hypocritical type is also of note.

When Vladina approached Malrenpar's circle of cohorts, Malrenpar smiled broadly and insincerely with what she imagined was a winning 'studly' showing of her discolored teeth from years of smoking cigarettes, weed and 'fweed' (fake weed). Vladina was well over a foot taller than Malrenpar, yet Malrenpar was so cocky that she thought she could easily overpower Vladina with her redneck charm and quite limited physical and mental strength. Vladina let her think that, enjoying the process...

Vladina asked Malrenpar and her colluders what they had planned for the rest of the night. They, of course, didn't say they were planning on setting up false sites to try and extort money from Malrenpar's ex, so they said they were going to just 'chill' at Derdy Assley's place (Malrenpar's main colluder and a fugly femme Malrenpar frequently hooked up with for grotesque sexual interaction). Wanna tag along,

Malrenpar asked, eying what she took to be the finest femme she'd ever seen, up and down overtly.

Vladina smiled, careful to keep her fangs retracted. Sure thing, she offered, in a voice like dark honey, closing her thick lashes slowly and cutting her eyes coquettishly. Funny how close malice and flirtation can present at times.

When the corrupt group led by Malrenpar was about a quarter mile from the church, having littered the ground with their church service fliers along the way not caring in the least about Mother Nature's sacred ground, they'd arrived in the farthest corner away from the church in the parking lot. They planned on smoking some fweed there safely away from the senior minister's view. It was now nighttime, and Vladina and Juracia could wait no longer to unleash the deserving carnage. Malrenpar mistakenly set aside her fweed to reach in for an ill-begotten kiss and grope of the amble cleavage rising steadily and seductively from the Gothic Corset Vladina was wearing. The imbecile

Malrenpar supposed erroneously that Vladina must want it from the way she was dressed, and Malrenpar was frozen in death for quite some time with a look of horror mixed with surprise when Vladina freed Juracia from her scabbard and beheaded Malrenpar with one fell swoop. It could be argued that Malrenpar should have suffered a longer more painful death, but Juracia was thirsty! Vladina quickly positioned Juracia between two large rocks and let her drink from Malrenpar's blood running down the bloodlet after she spiked Malrenpar's head on the tip of Juracia's blade. As for Malrenpar's criminal conspirators...Vladina killed them where they stood before they could turn away from the horror of seeing their cohort Malrenpar beheaded. Later, after Vladina had drained all of Malrenpar's former posse, which had stained a large section of the parking lot crimson in the process, she removed Malrenpar's disgusting deceased head from Juracia's tip to spike it on its new home atop the spire part of the Baptist church steeple for all to see for some time.

In fact, it was weeks before the church could hire a crew to remove it, so Malrenpar's head just decomposed for all who passed by to see. That is, the rotting parts that weren't picked at already by the turkey buzzards.

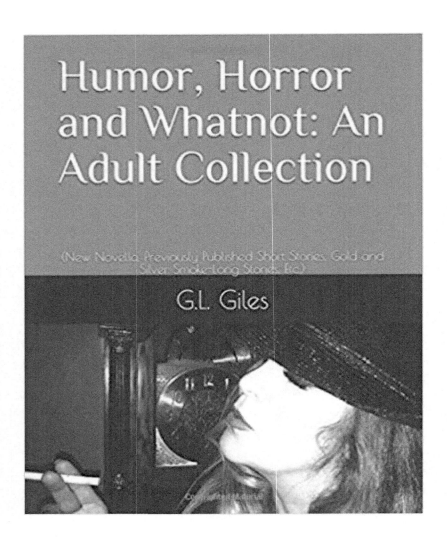

Humor, Horror and Whatnot: An Adult Collection

(New Novella, Previously Published Short Stories, Gold and Silver Smoke-Long Stories, Etc.)

G.L. Giles

Praise for G.L. Giles's "Humor, Horror and Whatnot":

"A Variety Show in Book Form: I love anything by G.L. Giles, as I have been following her writings, books and blogs- and whatnot!-for years. HUMOR, HORROR AND WHATNOT is a wildly funny and thought-provoking compendium that delivers right from the start with the short and sweet 4:20 (those in the know, know what that means…but what does a zombie with the munchies do? Hmm?). Some of these saucy stories would be right at home between the pages of 50s and 60s lad mags---they'd often run risqué but funny fiction alongside the cheesecake photos. HUMOR, HORROR AND WHATNOT is a great Halloween gift (it costs about the same as that bottle of wine you would be taking to the party and is a lot cooler) but it's a good book for anytime. I love the layout of these stories, because you can hunt-and-peck and are bound to land on something awesome no matter where you land.

Staci Layne Wilson, author of "Keepsakes"

"Darkly humorous and wildly original: Humor, Horror and Whatnot: An Adult Collection is a witty breath of fresh air about the complexity of romantic relationships, the unseen and supernatural world, zombies, vampires (some of them the bad relationship kind), with a dash of poetry and original photography…offering a tongue in cheek look at southern life and the eccentric characters that have come to personify the Deep South for many people.

The size is more traditional coffee table book than typical novel or anthology. At first I wasn't sure if I liked it, but now since the book is perched on my coffee table to read with a glass of wine after a long day…it's a match made in book heaven.

It's also literary in the sense that the author breaks a lot of writing "rules," and not only makes this form of exploration seem effortless, but it's also a lot of fun too.

The Upsurge is a horror story about dull-witted Southern zombies (with the best Lowcountry accent ever!) It's written without any quotation marks to mark the dialogue. This is a new style of writing, gaining in popularity and it feels very experimental, but once I got used to it, I really enjoyed it. You might think it would be impossible to follow along, but it was well written, darkly humorous, and thankfully not too gory. The fact that only vegetarians are spared being eaten by the undead inhabitants of Edisto Island during Hurricane Willa is totally hilarious. Yet another reason to go vegan! The zombies, like many modern Americans, will avoid eating their broccoli at all costs! LOL

A few lines I really enjoyed:

"My brother and I had never studied anything as complex as String Theory, so the idea of other worlds in other dimensions never even crossed our minds."
–Extreme Wards

"Damn he's lucky," I whispered to my wife.

"So's she," I was surprised to hear my butch wife say. "What?! I can't be an enlightened wo-man of the new millennium?!" she teased, her deep blue eyes dancing with devilry. –Along Came Polly Amery

There are a few dark and sexy short stories, short poems filled with yearning or passion which feel much like guitar riffs or songs, they all have a distinct flavor to them that flow into each other and move you in remembrance of single life or younger days or say to yourself, "Wow, so I'm not the only one?" The stories are revealing, brave and totally original.

This is a grown up collection you will enjoy reading again and again with short and longer text that will entertain the heck out of you, spark your imagination and if you're anything like me, the dark humor will make you laugh out loud too.

Bibiana Krall, author of "The Soul Keeper"

A Penchant for the Darkly Delightful: G.L. Giles has a penchant for the darkly delightful and stories full of eccentric and interesting characters. This collection features lyrics, poetry, short and long stories that dip into the darkness with an intelligent dark humor. You'll find cats who walk upright on hind legs and speak eloquent English, even ones ruling the world over human beings in a parallel universe. Common themes or subjects include vegetarians, animal rights, vampires, zombies and alternate lifestyles. One story features a brilliant Goth girl who abhors the mundane. Another story about zombies features two types of undead: Decomps and Shedders. Giles sets this tale in the Lowcountry of South Carolina, giving it the perfect local flavor. In a move toward experimentalism, she heads each chapter with the characters' points-of-view and tells their story in their own personal voice. The diverse and fascinating characters make each story come alive. Giles' voice and particular humor will keep readers riveted to the page. This example from her zombie tale "The Upsurge" gives a taste of what G.L. Giles has to offer: "Being a purveyor of memento mori he remembers that all have to die…even if it's twice, he thinks grimly." I can't recommend this collection highly enough!

Bryce Warren, author of "The Wretched"

.

Kitty's Parkour Palace

Feline Steward

Praise for Feline Steward's "Kitty's Parkour Palace":

"A whimsical and joyful tale for cool kids of any age!: The illustrations were what initially caught my eyes. They are creative, bright, and cheerful watercolors with a modern, fairy-tale vibe.

Kitty's Parkour Palace was told from the point of view of an awesome, very realistic feline named Anubis. I caught myself grinning, giggling and totally enjoying Anubis's exuberant voice, as the adventure unfolded. "A is for aerobics I love to do daily in my kitty cat palace…"

Wrapped inside the fun were clever clues about: respecting other people's private spaces, the importance of friendship, exalting in constant curiosity and simply enjoying life each day. I loved that the language was rendered to not speak down to children, instead it uplifted and the words were thoughtfully chosen to teach and improve the reader's vocabulary.

My favorite page was X. How many times as a kid did I spend a few hours trying to use X words in sentences? Come to think of it, maybe too many actually. I am still grinning from reading such a fun book to start my day!

I rarely read anything except philosophy and literary fiction, but this book made my day! I can't wait to get a copy for my niece and nephew. Thank you so much Feline Steward!

Bibiana Krall, author of "Moon Zinc"

Made in the USA
Coppell, TX
24 March 2020